Sherlock Holmes & The Case of the The Twain Papers

From The Notes of John H. Watson M.D.

Edited by

Roger Riccard

First published in 2014 by
The Irregular Special Press
for Baker Street Studios Ltd
Endeavour House
170 Woodland Road, Sawston
Cambridge, CB22 3DX, UK

ISBN: 1-901091-62-7 (10 digit)
ISBN: 978-1-901091-62-5 (13 digit)

Cover Concept: Antony J. Richards

Cover Illustration:

Typeset in 8/11/20pt Palatino

About the Author

Roger Riccard's family history has Scottish roots, which trace his lineage back to the Roses of Kilravock Castle near the village of Croy in Highland, Scotland. This British Isles ancestry encouraged his interest in the writings of Sir Arthur Conan Doyle at an early age. As the author of *Sherlock Holmes & The Case of the Poisoned Lilly*, (Baker Street Studios Ltd, June 2012) he was well received:

"Roger Riccard is an extremely good pastiche writer. Personally, I think the best since the late Val Andrews passed over Reichenbach."

Joel Senter – Publisher, Sherlockian E-Times

His Bachelor degrees in Journalism and History have served him well in his road to authorship. Now from his home in the suburbs of Los Angeles, California U.S.A., he has once again taken pen in hand, to compose his second foray into the world of the Baker Street sleuth, with *Sherlock Holmes and the Case of the Twain Papers*.

Preface

With the 2010 publication of Mark Twain's autobiography, the story which follows can now be told. Samuel L. Clemens' insistence that his autobiographical work remain unpublished until 100 years after his death has heretofore made it morally, if not legally, contingent that Doctor Watson's notes regarding Holmes involvement with the Clemens case should remain unpublished as well.

Clemens made several false starts in attempting to write down his autobiography. He did not reach his final format until 1906. However, there were copious notes from those previous starts, dating back as early as 1870. Many of these segments found their way into his final work, while others he chose not to include. When one reads the work today, it is easy to see why he insisted upon the century-long wait. It is also understandable why some people, or entities of his time, might not wish to see the work brought into the public eye.

Once again the trunk inherited by my grandmother from her aunt on the Hudson side of the family has revealed a treasure trove of Dr. Watson's jottings and I have attempted to organize them into this story form so that you may enjoy *Sherlock Holmes & The Case of the Twain Papers.*

Roger Riccard
Los Angeles
California
U.S.A.

To my Rosilyn.
Whose love made my life begin

Acknowledgement

Thank you to Joel and Carolyn Senter, 'Those Sherlock Holmes people in Cincinnati', for their advice, encouragement and tireless efforts in publishing the Sherlockian E-Times.

www.sherlock-holmes.com

Chapter One

In many circles of British society a great sigh of relief emanated with the passage of the New Year into the twentieth century. From my study of history I have found that the 'doomsday' predictions of philosophers and fanatics always increase when a century turns over. The Year 1900 was no exception. It always amazes me that such people believe that the Creator of the universe would align His actions with the Gregorian calendar.

The case which follows must reside in my files for yet another hundred years after the death of the victim. Provided the doomsayers are also wrong about the year 2000, and my writings about my celebrated friend, Mr. Sherlock Holmes, survive another century, then this case may prove of interest to those of that future era.

*****

It was Saturday, the sixth of January. We were having a quiet celebration of Sherlock Holmes' birthday in our dwellings at 221B Baker Street. Outside there was a light sprinkling of rain. In contrast to the gloomy winter's day, a hearty breakfast, provided by Mrs. Hudson, in front of a comfortable fire, made for a cosy atmosphere.

Holmes tossed aside the last of the morning papers and settled down across the table from me stating, "Watson, the London criminal classes have become a lazy fraternity!"

"How do you mean, Holmes?" I responded.

"Apparently they have chosen to sit by the fire in their abodes and stay warm and dry, rather than ply their trade in this miserable rain which has dampened the city for the past week."

"Surely that cannot be a bad thing," I countered.

He answered, somewhat belligerently, "My profession is dependent upon theirs and I am stagnating at their lack of initiative!" Realizing the implications of his statement, he reluctantly added, "Although, I will allow that London's would-be victims are better off."

His mood threatened to dampen our celebration, so I decided not to wait any longer before presenting his gift. Resigning, reluctantly, from the few titbits remaining of my ham and eggs, I left the table and retrieved a box from my room.

"Happy birthday, Holmes!" I exclaimed upon my return.

He took the bundle from me with a murmured 'Thank you' and set it down next to his plate. "You always remember, old friend. As little as I care for such celebrations, I confess that this symbolism of your friendship is welcome all the same."

"Then by all means, open it," I encouraged.

The box was fairly large and Holmes methodically cut its strings and removed the wrapping paper.

Upon opening it he pulled out what would have seemed a strange contraption to the average citizen. It was a miniature wooden door, eighteen inches tall and a foot wide, set on a heavy metal base. Along its edge there were five separate locking door handles of various styles.

"Upon my word, Watson, where did you get this device?" he enquired.

"A legitimate question, Holmes; unfortunately I would have to give you an illegitimate answer, as these are only supposed to be sold to licensed locksmiths. Oh, by the way," I continued, pulling another present from my pocket, "these go with it."

He took the packet from my extended hand and promptly removed the wrapping. Inside there was a black leather case which, upon opening, revealed multiple metal objects. These were, in fact, lock picks and skeleton keys of various styles.

"Watson, you have outdone yourself!" he exclaimed.

"I knew that your old set was becoming outdated with these new locking devices." I replied and continued *sotto voce*, "I am assured, by a certain gentleman of our acquaintance, that you now have the latest tools of the trade, as well as the locks to practice on."

"Oh my, Watson, how I have corrupted you! Your foray into the underworld of London to obtain these items is surely not what you must have expected when you received your medical degree."

"I assure you, Holmes," I replied, "I would not have traded these last two decades of our friendship, and adventures, for anything."

Just then Mrs. Hudson, with that incredible timing of her landlady's instincts, walked in with a small birthday cake.

"Happy birthday, Mr. Holmes!" she announced. She set the cake on the table with a single burning candle which Holmes promptly blew out.

"Thank you, Mrs. Hudson," he said, with a nod in her direction.

"My pleasure, Mr. Holmes," she replied. "Oh, you also have a gentleman waiting downstairs. I wouldn't let him come up unannounced. Here is his card. He appears to be an American from his accent. An older man."

"How interesting," he answered, scrutinizing the card. "Please show the gentleman up."

As she left the room Holmes turned to me, "You see, Watson, I have even turned our long-suffering landlady into an observer. I had no idea how much my life has affected those around me."

"All for the better, Holmes I assure you. Who is your potential client?"

"Someone with whom you share a literary penchant, Doctor," he answered and handed me the card.

Just as I was reading it the man himself appeared in our doorway. He was wearing a black suit, grey overcoat and a broad brimmed hat to dispel the damp weather, but the face underneath was unmistakable. The bushy moustache and the great mane of grey/white hair were synonymous with the most famous American in London at the moment.

"Samuel Clemens!" cried Holmes, in welcome to our visitor. "Come in, sir. This is indeed a pleasant surprise."

Clemens[1] handed his hat and overcoat to me as I introduced myself.

"Doctor Watson," he said, shaking my hand vigorously, "it is indeed a great delight to meet you, sir. I must tell you that I am a passionate fan of your work. Why, there is no English writer whose stories I enjoy more than those that have flowed from your pen to our shores. I have missed your writings terribly these past few years, often contemplating the possibility that there might be more cases hidden in some file box somewhere, a'waitin' an appropriate mourning period before resurrectin' the memory of your famous friend."

His voice was somewhat high-pitched and his speech consisted of a duet of Southern drawl and Yankee twang, an oddly pleasant combination.

"It is an honour to be recognized by so famous an author as yourself, sir," I replied modestly.

"And now," the garrulous old gentleman continued, "I find your friend has no need of resurrection, for there he sits, in all his detective glory.

"You, Mr. Holmes," he said, turning toward my companion "have been hiding from the public far too long, leastwise, the American public. Why I thought your body

---

[1] Samuel Clemens, a.k.a. Mark Twain, was famous for wearing white suits. However, the generally accepted theory is that he did not start wearing them on a regular basis until after his wife, Olivia, had passed away in 1904. He later explained to journalists why he wore white: "I have found that when a man reaches the advanced age of 71 years, as I have, the continual sight of drab clothing is likely to have a depressing effect upon him. Light-coloured clothing is more pleasing to the eye and enlivens the spirit."

permanently consigned to the bottom of Reichenbach Falls until I talked to a police inspector yesterday."

Holmes smiled and replied, as he stood and shook Clemens hand, "To quote you sir, 'The report of my death was an exaggeration'.[2] But come, sit down and tell us what brings you to our humble home."

Spying the birthday cake Clemens remarked, "I don't wish to interrupt your celebration, gentlemen, for I am a firm believer in celebrations. Yes, sir, especially birthdays, of which I have engaged in sixty-four such ceremonials. But I thought I might solicit your services before the trail grew cold."

"Tut, tut, Clemens, if you have brought me a case it would be a very welcome birthday present."

"Thank you, Mr. Holmes. But you have my curiosity up. Dr. Watson hasn't written anything about you for five or six years now.[3] Have one, or both of you, retired?"

Holmes replied, "On the contrary, I have remained quite active in my work since I returned from my travels in '94, although, as they say on the stage, I am 'at liberty' at the moment. I have restrained the doctor from publishing my cases due to their most unfortunate effect on my true work."

"Unfortunate effects?" queried the author. "I would think the lack of publicity would be the most unfortunate of effects, Mr. Holmes. I would wager you've missed many a case because people think you're deceased. I am a very firm believer in publicity, myself. I have been known to take out advertisements in the newspapers and magazines, just to make sure that I am properly recognized by the public, don't you see. For who else knows better than myself what I am about?"

At this point I spoke up, "In fact, Mr. Clemens, Holmes feels he was getting too much publicity. As much as I miss the writing, I have kept notes on the cases so that they can be

---

[2] In 1897, while he was in England, it was erroneously reported in America that 'Mark Twain' had died.
[3] Actually, none since 1893's *The Final Problem*

published at some future date. Although failing memory may confuse the cases by then." I added, with a trace of piquancy.

"I invented a game once," remarked the American, "which was designed to help folks' memory. Patented it too, back in '85. *Mark Twain's Memory Builder*, I called it. It was supposed to help people remember significant historical facts and dates."

"Really?" I responded, "I had no idea."

He waved his hand nonchalantly, "Nothing came of it, Doctor. According to its critics I had made the instructions too complicated to remember how to play!"

I chortled, "Well perhaps I should try it. Just to make sure I don't distort the facts whenever I write up my notes for publication."

"Distorting the cases with romanticized dash and falderal was already a problem," retorted Holmes, as he steepled his fingers. "Thanks to my friend's foray into the popular press, I was receiving dozens of callers and scores of letters every week, seeking my assistance to find a missing cat, or trace down a misplaced bill or take action against some perceived radical group that did not subscribe to a person's ideals. There was even one crackpot who wanted me to prove that he was the true heir to Napoleon and restore him to the throne of France."

Clemens smiled, "I can certainly understand why you would want to turn down that case Mr. Holmes. The man who exposes a fool's folly is never appreciated by the fool. Of course, if he fails to persuade the fool of the error of his ways, then who becomes more the fool? The original fool, or the supposedly intelligent man who fails to dissuade the foolishness? It is a conundrum that I, myself choose to avoid. Excepting when the foolishness is my own, of course."

Then, in a more serious tone, he continued, "But surely, sir, you do the Doctor an injustice. The exercise of an extraordinary gift is the supremest pleasure in life, as you should well know. You have your cases, but poor Watson here, has been shackled from using his gift of writing. Depriving the masses from the entertainments of his work, and himself of the plaudits and accolades he so richly deserves."

"I am not interested in the entertainments of the masses. I seek the resolution of problems and the dispensing of justice," replied Holmes.

Clemens, sensing that he had trespassed into an old argument of ours, changed the subject.

"Well, I do have a problem, Mr. Holmes, and I hope the resolution will exercise your gift to some extent, so that you will not feel put upon by an old fool."

"Forgive me, Mr. Clemens," said the detective, contritely. "I suppose the acknowledgement of another passing year and the lack of work in this miserable weather has made me a bit testy. Pray, state your problem."

"It may not seem much to you, Mr. Holmes. In fact, it may better gather the sympathies of Dr. Watson here. But, the truth of the matter is, someone has stolen my life."

Chapter Two

In the silence that followed this extraordinary statement, Clemens pulled out his cigar case and quietly asked, "Do y'all mind if I smoke, gentlemen?"

"By no means," said Holmes, and proceeded to stuff his own pipe from the Persian slipper. I decided to forgo any tobacco for the moment. Instead I pulled out my notebook and pencil and leaned forward to make sure I heard every word.

"As I do not believe in ghosts, I assume you have an explanation for that remark," stated Holmes.

Pointing his cigar between his thumb and forefinger at the detective, Clemens replied, "When it comes to the existence of ghosts I'm not sure I agree with you, sir. However, the 'life' I refer to is my collection of notes and manuscripts that I have been attempting to organize into my autobiography."

"I see," puffed Holmes through the blue haze that had begun to gather around his head. "Just when did this remarkable theft occur?"

"Near as I can figure, sometime between six o'clock Thursday evening and ten o'clock yesterday morning."

Holmes glanced at me and indicated that I should make note of the time, then continued.

"And where were these papers kept?"

Clemens waved his cigar, dispensing a rather foul odour throughout the room, "My family and I are currently stayin' at the Langham Hotel. These particular papers were in the study of my suite there."

"Very well then!" said Holmes rising, "We should go examine the scene of the crime as quickly as possible before it becomes further contaminated."

"I'd appreciate your efforts, Mr. Holmes," replied the American. "Inspector Hopkins has blocked off the room, after he examined it yesterday. It was only after he mentioned that he might send for you that I learned you were still alive. Now I thought this a most fortuitous circumstance, and, being a notoriously curious person myself, I naturally desired to see the famous 221B Baker Street. So, of course, I volunteered to come ask you in person this morning, if you would be so kind as to assist him in my little predicament."

"Then we shall accompany you at once. Agreed, Watson?"

"Most assuredly, Holmes," I answered, tucking my pencil and notebook into my pocket and rising to retrieve my overcoat, bowler and umbrella. Soon we were in a carriage provided to Mr. Clemens by the hotel and rumbling southward to that grand establishment. Had the weather been more hospitable we could have easily walked, for the Langham is but a mile or so from Baker Street. However, taking the carriage also led to the happy circumstance of Mr. Clemens refraining from further smoking what he apparently believed passed for cigars. While I have been subject to many of Holmes' experiments in foreign tobacco, never have my olfactory senses been assaulted by such a malodorous stench as that emanating from the famous author's stogie.

We quickly approached the towering architectural structure with its unique shapes and great height. Only thirty-seven years ago, the foundation stone of The Langham Hotel had been laid. From the outset many thought the proposed project was too ambitious to be a success. However, on Saturday the 10th of June 1865, The Langham enjoyed its grand opening, enchanting the Prince of Wales and Victorian high society. It became London's first Grand Hotel, rising over six storeys above the streets in the city's West End.

The driver deposited us at the prominent covered archway with its multiple columns and bright chandelier, bearing its light even now against the gloom of the day and inviting all into the glamour of its lobby.

We took the lift up to the fourth floor, where Clemens' suite was under the perusal of Inspector Stanley Hopkins. Hopkins, unlike some at Scotland Yard, was always welcoming of Holmes on a case and attempted to emulate the great detective's methods since their first association in 1894[1].

He brightened at our approach and greeted Holmes warmly. "Mr. Holmes, it is good of you to come." With a smiling nod to me, and a 'Hello, Dr. Watson,' he turned back to my companion, "I've kept the scene as intact as possible for you. Of course there are such of my footprints as were necessary for the initial investigation, but I believe I've discovered those of our burglar near the window where the carpet was wet from the rain pouring in through the broken glass. There do not seem to be any fingerprints so it's likely the culprit wore gloves."

"Excellent, Hopkins," said Holmes, removing his own gloves and setting them aside with his hat and coat on a nearby chair. We followed Hopkins into the section of the suite that Clemens used as a study. Holmes held his hands out, indicating that we should stay back. He then placed his open hands aside his eyes and slowly pivoted his vision back and forth across the scene.

Dropping to his knees, he focused his vision across the carpeting. At which point Clemens whispered to me, "This is

---

[1] *The Adventure of the Golden Pince-Nez*

fascinating, Doctor. I had always thought you exaggerated a bit when describing Holmes' antics at assessing a crime scene, but, now I see, you were perfectly accurate."

"Yes," I replied quietly, "Holmes does indeed contort into some strange positions to ascertain what physical clues may be available. I've seen him scamper across rooftops and climb down drain pipes, just to satisfy himself on certain possibilities."

At this point Holmes rose to one knee and addressed our client. "The papers were kept in a small briefcase with a bent left hinge, here under the desk?"

"Yes, indeed, Mr. Holmes" replied Clemens. 'The hinge was bent some years ago while we were in Italy. Now *that* is some country for ..."

Waving his hand in interruption, Holmes pointed directly at Clemens, which had the amazing effect of silencing the loquacious gentleman.

From this position he asked, "This case certainly could not have contained all the jottings of your lifetime. You are far too prolific a note taker to have your adventures confined to so small a container."

"You are correct, sir. The majority of my notes are still in files in Connecticut. I have just enough here to prod my memory, especially of my previous visit to your fair country."

Holmes nodded and then crawled his way across toward the French doors, which opened onto the fire escape, where a hole in one of the panes near the latch advertised the method of entry for Clemens' intruder. Here he spent considerable time studying the wet carpet with his magnifying glass. He rose to a crouch and made a note on a scrap of paper retrieved from his waistcoat pocket. He then proceeded to study the neat hole made in the window pane and the latch itself. The opening had apparently been cut with a glass cutter, as it was a perfect semi-circle removing nearly half the square pane and allowing room enough for a gloved hand to reach the door latch. The pane itself lay on the carpet inside the room and was subjected to Holmes' magnifier. Again he scribbled a note to himself.

Satisfied, he then opened the door and peered out onto the fire escape. Stepping gingerly out onto the platform he bent to examine the railing and steps. He plucked something off the corner of the railing going down and stuffed it into an envelope drawn from inside his coat. He then examined the guard rail of the platform directly outside the room with his magnifying lens and nodded abstractly. He gave a cursory glance at the railing coming down from the floor above and shook his head.

He then returned to the room carefully, stepping over the footprints by the window, and retreated across the room to examine the entrance door's lock.

Satisfied, he turned to Clemens, who had, by this time, lowered his aging body into a chair on the opposite side of the room and out of the way of Holmes' gyrations.

"What time were you out of the room on Thursday night?" he asked.

Removing a 'fresh' cigar from his mouth the author replied, "We all left to enjoy dinner and attend a play at the Lyceum Theatre at six o'clock.

"It was one of them Shakespearean plays, you understand. Well, of course you do. It's too bad my Americanized understanding of the English language left me somewhat dazed and confused. How-some-ever, the actors were mighty fine at any rate. Everyone seemed to know their lines, antiquated as they might have been, and the action on stage was well performed. We all returned, after some pleasant post-play refreshments, just before midnight."

"And you did not notice whether the suitcase was in place, or if there was a draft from the window?"

"No, Mr. Holmes. We were mighty tired by that point and the drapes were closed so we just went straight off to bed. It wasn't 'til ten the next morning that I found the hole in the window when I opened the drapes to catch the morning sun. I called down to report it to the front desk and after that, I conducted a search of the place to see if anything were missing. It was then I discovered my papers were gone."

"And nothing else has been taken?"

"Not a thing," he replied.

"What do you think, Mr. Holmes?" asked the Scotland Yarder.

"This was no simple snoozer[2], Hopkins. It was carefully planned and specifically targeted Clemens' papers. The time taken to set this scene was far too long to risk occurrence while the family slept in the next room. This means you can narrow the time frame to that in which the family was gone. The perpetrator knew he would have at least four hours while the Clemens were out, if he were aware of their dinner and theatre plans and travel time to each and back."

"What do you mean 'set the scene', Holmes?" I asked.

In response, Holmes turned to our client and enquired, "Sir, you are one of the great storytellers of the English

---

[2] Snoozer – British term for 'one who steals items from hotel rooms, often while guests are asleep'.

language. What would be your version of what has occurred here?"

"Well, Mr. Holmes, I hardly think many of your countrymen would consider my stories to be written in English," he chuckled, "But I believe someone came in, either up or down the fire escape, cut a hole in the glass so as to not make any noise, went on to search the room 'til he found what he was a-lookin' for, and left the same way."

"And why, do you suppose, the thief stole just that particular briefcase?" Holmes prodded.

Hopkins spoke up and replied, "Our theory is that he heard something and was scared off before he could finish the job."

"No, no, Hopkins it will not do!" responded my friend. "The care exercised in planting false clues would have required foresight and careful manipulation. This thief was after Clemens' papers and nothing more. It may be his one mistake that he did not steal anything else to make it appear to be an ordinary burglary."

"*Planted* clues, Holmes?" I questioned.

"The glass in the door was cut from the inside: the bevelling from the cut shows as much, as does the fact that the glass is intact on the floor, where it was placed, after being removed by a suction cup device. Had it been pushed in from the outside it would have fallen and likely either cracked or broken. Also there are no smears of hand or glove on the pane opposite the latch. The positioning of that latch would have required a person reaching in from the outside to at least have brushed the other glass when opening the door.

"The paint on the railings outside is flaking and showing signs of rust but there is no indication of a hand being placed anywhere on them, either up or down. Yet there was a scrap of cloth conveniently caught on the lower railing. Obviously meant to lead the police to assume the culprit descended the fire escape to take his flight. I did, however, find a section of the railing, opposite to the stairs, where the rust and flaking paint were scraped away, likely by someone leaning over to lower the case to an accomplice in the alley.

"The shoeprint in the wet carpeting is conveniently leading out, but it is curiously in the wrong position for anyone opening the door from the inside. Also, all the footprints of this size, which you will note are rather large, have an unusual weight distribution. See how the toe barely makes a mark, while the centre of the print is easily distinguishable."

"What does that mean, Holmes? "I queried.

"Perhaps it is a deformity, perhaps something else. It is unusual and that makes it noteworthy.

"Finally, we have the entrance from the hall. The lock is of a newer variety and was recently installed. There are no scratches on the edge of the keyhole to indicate that the lock was picked. So we have someone with access to a key or a twirler[3] with a very steady hand."

At this point our American friend rose out of his chair and applauded.

"Bravo, Mr. Holmes!" he cried. "I got to say seeing you in action is a treat worthy of any stage performance I have ever come across. Well done!"

"Elementary observation and deduction, Mr. Clemens," Holmes replied. "The real question before us is, 'Why did someone want to steal the notes for your autobiography?'"

---

[3] Twirler – Someone who picks locks using skeleton keys.

Chapter Three

By this time the cold weather had taken its toll on my old Afghan war wound and I deposited myself on the settee opposite to the chair Clemens occupied. I had no sooner sat down than a large blue/gray feline jumped into my lap and lay there, staring up with its green eyes, seemingly demanding to be petted.

"Well, hello there!" I said as I scratched behind its ears and down its soft long back. "Who might you be?"

"That," answered Clemens, "is General Grant. Least that's what we call him. Seems he came with the room and, as you can see, he is a very pleasant companion, as well as an excellent mouser."

"Seems a bit odd to name a cat after a former president," said Hopkins. "I mean, isn't that a bit insulting?"

"I'm sure the cat doesn't mind," replied the American.

"I meant to President Grant," replied the Inspector, patiently.

"Oh, Ulysses is an old friend of mine," answered Clemens. "He would take it as a compliment I'm sure. After all, of all God's creatures there is only one that cannot be made the slave of the lash. That one is the cat. If man could be crossed with the cat it would improve man, but it would deteriorate the cat. Which is why, I suppose, that cats have never allowed it to happen."

"Well said, Mr. Clemens," remarked Sherlock Holmes, "but now as to motive for the theft of your documents ...?"

"Ah, yes. Well, I'm sure I don't have to tell you, Mr. Holmes, that in my experience there are plenty of possible motives for any thievery. Now about my notes, there could be collectors out there who have a misplaced opinion of the value of my works and might want to have them as part of an accumulation of 19th century Americana."

"You underestimate yourself, sir," replied the detective. "That is a definite possibility. There is also the question of ransom. I assume there has been no demand from the thief?"

"None, Mr. Holmes," answered Hopkins.

"What about using them for blackmail purposes?" I interjected.

"I suppose there could be some prospect in that," my fellow author nodded, thoughtfully. "But, off the top of my head, I can't hardly think of anything in those particular notes that could bring about such a desperate and despicable action."

"That leads us to the possibility of revenge," Holmes stated, as he lit a cigarette. The lighting of the match perked up the cat in my lap and he immediately jumped down and sulked to a safe spot under the desk.

"The General doesn't take much to fire," remarked Clemens. "Every time I light a cigar he hightails it under some piece of furniture or t'other."

Holmes paused and digested that remark, then spoke up. "Our thief could also be playing with fire."

"How do you mean, Mr. Holmes?" asked Hopkins.

"He hasn't asked for a ransom, which is always risky in making the exchange at any rate. If he sells them on the open market it would surely lead back to him, since the papers of such a famous living author are bound to attract attention. If his purpose was to destroy them, then our cause is lost, for surely he would have done so by now. If he is a mere collector then it could be years before his collection is open to the public eye, likely at his own death. But, if he is using the information in them for the blackmail of some individual other than you, Mr. Clemens, it could be most difficult to trace, unless you can think of some information in those papers that might be worthy of such an effort."

The last remark was addressed to Clemens who nodded and drawled, "I'll certainly think on it, Mr. Holmes, but off the top of my head there ain't likely to be anything there. I do have one other thought though."

"What's that, sir?" queried Holmes

"When I was here in London, back in '73, a fellow came to me and my friends in absolute destitution. His clothes were threadbare and his family was just a-starvin'. He said he was a writer, just startin' out. He asked my companions for some help in loaning him money for his poor kinfolk. They gave him some and they also connected him to a publisher. He ended up sellin' his first story for three guineas. We only found out later that the story he submitted, and got paid for mind you, was in fact *Jim Wolf and the Cats*. That happened to be my story, which I had published in the United States back in 1867. So it's just possible that this here thief could be someone who is out for material to publish under his own name."

"An interesting hypothesis, Mr. Clemens," responded my friend.

At this I spoke up, "Holmes, it has also happened to me, if you remember. In the absence of publishing your adventures in recent years a number of imitators have tried to build upon those first few stories just by changing our names. Just think if they actually had access to your case files."

"I see your point, Watson," he replied, "although the public interest in your romanticized tales has always surprised me."

"Just hold on there, Mr. Holmes," cried Clemens. "I can promise you that interest in more adventures of yours would be even greater than any works I might come up with. Why, I tried my hand at a detective story once, with Tom Sawyer.[1] I took real facts and just fictionalized 'em. It's the real

---

[1] *Tom Sawyer, Detective* - 1896

possibility of cases that makes 'em so interestin' to the general public, don't you know ?"

"Well, you are entitled to your opinion," replied my friend. Turning to Hopkins he enquired, "Inspector, I assume you have questioned hotel management and staff?"

"I have had a discussion with the manager, Mr. Holmes," Hopkins answered. "I was planning on questioning the night staff when they came in to work later."

"That may be too late, if one of them is the thief he may have already flown. You did not think to send officers around to their homes?"

Feeling a bit like on the receiving end of a lecture, the Inspector answered defensively, "I did not think it necessary. The entire staff that was working on Thursday night showed up for work on Friday as well. I assumed that if our thief was among them he was not likely to return to the scene and risk exposure."

Holmes pondered that and replied, "Hmm, yes. The thief would have to be bold indeed to return. Still I should like to speak with the manager and satisfy myself on a few points. Will you join me, Inspector?"

Whether he realized it or not, Hopkins had just received what, for Holmes, might be considered an apology for his brusque statement. The Scotland Yarder agreed to accompany the detective.

"Have you completed your examination of the room, then?" he asked.

"Yes, I believe we have learned all we can here," replied Holmes.

Thus the three of us excused ourselves from Clemens' company and returned to the ground floor to glean what we could from the Langham's manager.

*****

As the lift doors opened to the lobby and we followed Hopkins toward the manager's office, I suddenly heard my name called.

"John? Dr. Watson!"

I turned and saw a familiar face, though not from recent experience. It was a tall blonde woman near forty years of age. She was dressed in a light grey skirt and jacket over a Kelly green blouse. Her hat was fashioned after a man's bowler with matching green hatband and ribbon trailing behind. Her hazel eyes shone in recognition when I turned and a smile broadened her pleasant cheeks.

Beside her stood a younger woman of about twenty, with long brown curls falling below her bonnet and cascading down her red plaid dress with white ruffles at the collar and cuffs. Hanging a bit behind was a youth of about sixteen or seventeen, but tall for his age. In fact he was as tall as I and as they approached his appearance was the most remarkable to my sight.

"Adelaide? Adelaide Savage?" I queried. "Oh, and this cannot possibly be young George!"

The lady held her hand out to me and I brushed the back of it gently with a proper kiss. "John, it is so good to see you again. Yes this is George."

Holmes had stopped to see what had drawn my attention. Recognizing Mrs. Savage, he greeted her politely and excused himself, though he bade me stay while he and Hopkins continued on.

The youth shook my extended hand heartily. "It is a pleasure to see you, sir." He had the blue grey eyes and handsome face of his father. His build was lean, but there was strength in that handshake that was beyond his years.

"And of course, this is Marina." Mrs. Savage added, indicating the young lady as her daughter.

I bowed over the girl's extended hand and looked into a pair of inquisitive brown eyes, obviously searching her memory for my image. I had been quite involved in the care of the Savages at the time Victor Savage had been murdered by his uncle, Mr. Culverton Smith, by way of an exotic poison. Smith then evicted the widow and her children from the estate, as he was next in line by succession. It had occurred ten years earlier and I had not as yet published the story for the sake of Mrs. Savage and her children.[2] Holmes, of course, solved the case and proved Smith as the killer through an ingenious deception of his own.

The last time I had seen the Savage family had been at my wife's funeral. I found it little wonder that Marina, only twelve or so at that time, did not remember me. In fact, I was rather impressed that the younger George seemed to recognize me after what, to him, was nearly half a lifetime ago.

"What brings you to the City?" I enquired.

Beaming with pride and placing a hand upon her son's shoulder, she stated, "George will begin studying for a medical degree at the University of London next week."

"Well that *is* quite an accomplishment. I did not realize that the University was offering classes now. When I attended it was merely to sit for my doctor's exam." I answered. "Congratulations young man"

"Thank you, Doctor," he answered with some modesty. "The university just became a teaching school two years ago. I was lucky to be accepted."

"Have you decided upon a course of study?"

"I have taken an interest in veterinary medicine, what with the horses and dogs we have at home. If I have the aptitude for it, I think I would like to go into that field."

"Well, the country could certainly use some good veterinarians," I replied. "I wish you success, George."

Our conversation continued with catching up on the past few years and, I confess, it was a most pleasant interlude.

Holmes then stepped back out of the manager's office and caught my eye.

"I am afraid I must be going. Holmes and I are on a case."

"Of course," replied the comely widow, "But I do wish we could visit some more. We'll be here for a few more days. Perhaps you could join us for dinner some evening?"

---

[2] *The Adventure of the Dying Detective* would be published in 1913 with no mention of Mrs. Savage or her children. The first names used herein are from the Granada Television Production of Doyle's story © 1994.

"That would be my pleasure!" I found myself exclaiming, "When I know how our investigation is proceeding, I will try to arrange it."

"Excellent!" she responded, "We will look forward to it."

With a quick bow and a smile, I turned and followed Holmes, who was halfway through the lobby towards the entrance. I found it quite easy to catch up to him with no thought to the stiffness that the cold weather usually brings to my leg. My footsteps felt lighter than they had in many a year.

Chapter Four

As if in response to my mood, the rain had ceased and the clouds were breaking apart, allowing a few rays of sunshine to heat the streets and cause steam to rise from the warming pavement.

Holmes led the way for Hopkins and me around the side of the hotel and back into the alley that ran behind. As we turned the corner, he brought us to a stop and began examining the ground as we made our way to the base of the fire escape. Here he bent down and retrieved two cigarette butts, examined some footprints left in the mud and another strange mark, seemingly made by something round, approximately eighteen inches in diameter. He looked up and held his gloved hand high, brushing the brim of his Homburg, as if lining up with some point far up the wall.

Hopkins and I both strained our eyes in an attempt to ascertain what my friend was looking at when he suddenly spoke.

"Yes, it is as I surmised." Looking to the Scotland Yard Inspector he continued, "You are looking for two men, Hopkins. There was one who entered the room by way of the door and another, who waited here, to retrieve the case that was lowered by a strong fishing line from Clemens' room.

"This fellow," Holmes indicated by pointing to the ground, "wore military boots and smoked expensive

French cigarettes as he stood his post. He was a patient man, though he did not have to wait long. There is no evidence of his pacing about or leaning against the wall."

"But why wait here, Holmes?" replied the young inspector, "Why not ascend the fire escape and retrieve his ill-gotten gains and then make his escape back down again?"

"The railings are not meant for stealth, Inspector," answered the detective. "The metal is far too noisy for a quiet traverse. Also, it would take him past all the other floors below Clemens' room where he might be observed."

But, Holmes," I asked, "wouldn't the sight of the briefcase being lowered also be observable from the rooms below?"

"It could, Watson, but not as likely. The marks made were by the fishing line, on the railing outside our victim's room. They are on the far side of the fire escape platform, clearly out of direct sight from rooms below. One would almost have to be at the window looking out to see something travelling down the side. Considering that there is no view to enjoy, plus the inclement weather, the odds against the case being spotted were in our burglars' favour."

Satisfied with this explanation, Hopkins knelt down, pointing to the ground and enquired, "What of this circular indentation, Mr. Holmes?"

"That, my dear Inspector, is the bottom of a standard issue duffel bag, used no doubt, to transport the briefcase and line away unobserved. This may mean that our courier was in uniform so as not to draw attention to his load."

"A soldier then," said the Inspector.

"Not necessarily," replied Holmes. "There are many ways to obtain a military uniform without being on active duty."

Standing again, Hopkins made a note of this, "Anything else, Mr. Holmes?"

"I believe we've gleaned what we can for now, Inspector. I shall continue my enquiries and keep you apprised."

"Well, thank you then. I'll go write up my report and let you know if we turn anything up at the Yard."

We then returned to the front of the hotel and bade Hopkins farewell. On the ride home, Holmes filled me in on what had occurred in the hotel manager's office.

"The manager's name is Drysdale," Holmes informed me. "He's been in that post for six years. Married with four children, he is a large man of approximately six and one half feet and close to twenty stone. He is forty years of age and is well-to-do. Neither slovenly nor ostentatious, he is an efficient and friendly administrator who knows his staff quite well and is adamant in his assertion that none of them could be responsible for the theft of Clemens' papers. The door locks in the hotel were upgraded a year ago and the keys are well accounted for. The staff who were on duty during the evening of the theft will be coming in at 4:00 this afternoon and I shall return at that time to examine them."

Arriving at Baker Street we found Mrs. Hudson, taking advantage of our absence, airing out our sitting room and busily running a carpet sweeper across the rugs. The breakfast dishes were long since cleared and my present to Holmes lay neatly upon a fresh dark green tablecloth.

I removed my overcoat as we approached the fire to regain some warmth after our excursion. Holmes filled his pipe and I set match to a cigar that would hopefully erase the scent of Clemens' poisonous weed.

Holmes then proceeded to the table to examine the locks and picks I had procured for him.

"Would you care for lunch, gentlemen?" came the voice of our landlady from the doorway, "I've soup on the stove and there's ham left for sandwiches."

"Nothing for me, Mrs. Hudson," replied my friend. "I'll be off after this pipe. Watson," he continued. "After you've eaten, would you be so kind as to enquire of your gift supplier whether or not he is aware of any other such merchandise being acquired through the 'unconventional' channels he uses? It may provide us with a trail toward our thief."

"Certainly, Holmes," I answered. "Where are you off to?"

Exhaling a cloud of smoke he stuffed the new lock picks into his coat pocket and stated, "I am returning to the hotel to experiment upon the locks to Clemens' room, after which I shall speak with the night staff and, I hope, guests on the same floor near the scene of the crime. If you finish your errand quickly, I would appreciate you joining me there."

To Mrs. Hudson he announced, "I suspect we will be home for supper, but please take no offence if we are delayed."

Chapter Five

After a filling lunch, I again wrapped myself against the cold and ventured out on my mission.

I soon found myself back at Pawnbroker Maury's, the establishment where I had arranged for Holmes' birthday gift. It was run by a man of dubious reputation who had formerly been known as 'Maury the Bagger'. His assistance on a previous case of Holmes, one that I have not written but noted as "The Silver Fleece", had earned him a reprieve from the detective for his own involvement. He had taken his share of the reward money and purchased this pawn shop. The rows of goods stretched out before me like a farmer's newly ploughed field. They were filled with every imaginable sort of tool and appliance of varying quality, including some gimcrackery and bric-a-brac of dubious taste and usefulness.

Maury was seated at the counter next to the front door and greeted me warmly. "Afternoon, Doctor," the short man called, looking up from his newspaper. His dark, curly hair was starting to grey about the temples and his once lithe body was exhibiting a paunch from the idleness of middle age. "How'd your little surprise for Mr. Holmes work out?"

"Oh, he was quite pleased, Maury. Thank you. Actually that's what I've come to talk to you about."

"He don't know it was me what got it for you does he?"

"Oh no, I kept that part of our agreement. That's why I'm here alone. We are working on a case and he was curious as to who else may have obtained such items recently."

"Ah, Dr. Watson, I daresay there ain't a man in all London what could pull off what I did for you in obtaining them items."

"I see," I nodded.

"Of course," he reconsidered thoughtfully, "a true businessman of a certain type might go about his business undetected. I could look into it deeper if you like. Naturally it might require some expenses to grease a few blokes' palms...."

I took the hint and produced a fiver for his eyes to light upon. "Then grease away, my good man. Just keep our names out of it."

He snipped the bill from my hand with a quick flick of the wrist. "Not to fear there, Doctor, the name of 'Sherlock Holmes' would slam some of the doors I'll be knockin' on so fast that a hundred quid wouldn't budge 'em. You just give me two – no, no, tomorrow's Sunday. Make it three days and I'll have an answer for you."

"Very well," I replied and took my leave of his shop to rendezvous with Holmes at the Langham.

*****

The clouds that had retreated earlier were back with a vengeance as I departed my cab in front of that grand hotel. Those, in addition to the short winter days, were bringing about a darkness long before one would normally expect. The chill held the promise of snow rather than the rains London had suffered the previous week.

I strode through the lobby and spoke to the man at the front desk who informed me that Holmes was interviewing staff members in a small office just down the east hall.

As I entered the room, Holmes was standing behind the desk while a young woman in a maid's uniform sat opposite him in a chair. My friend acknowledged me with a glance as

40

the maid, a stout woman with short blonde hair and freckled cheeks, continued her statement.

"No, Mr. Holmes, I didn't notice any fishing line or odd pairs of shoes in any of the rooms on that floor. But then I only makes up the beds, you see, and change the towels. I don't go into the guests' closets, drawers or luggage. That's not allowed."

Holmes frowned and dismissed her with a "Thank you, Miss Day", and turned to me.

"Well, Watson, the day staff know nothing helpful and the night crew won't be on duty for another hour. How did your errand fare?"

I explained to him that it might take my source up to three days to ascertain if anyone else had procured the lock picks necessary.

"Three days, Watson! Our quarry could be halfway across Europe or on a ship to America! Ah, well, it's good that I also have the Baker Street Irregulars sniffing about. I've also sent a telegram to the manufacturer to ascertain if there have been any discrepancies in their inventory."

"What now then, Holmes?"

"Drysdale states that only two parties have checked out from the fourth floor since the night of the theft. Hopkins is looking into them, but I hold out little hope. They were a widow travelling with her son and a salesman who had only stopped for the one night en route to Edinburgh."

"Are you certain that our thief was a guest and that he was ensconced on the fourth floor, Holmes? Could he not have resided on some other floor or merely came in pretending to be a visitor to another guest?"

"I have not entirely dismissed those possibilities, Watson. However, no one would risk the testimony of a lift operator noting their exit onto the floor of the crime. The stairs, being at the far end of the hall, would subject them to possible witnesses for an unlikely length of exposure."

Continuing to play devil's advocate, I pressed him further. "What if they were disguised as a member of the hotel staff?" I posed.

41

"That thought has also entered my mind, old friend, and I will discuss it with the members of the evening staff shortly. For now I suggest we visit those guests sharing the fourth floor with Mr. Clemens to see if any further facts come to light."

"Surely Hopkins has questioned them already." I suggested.

"Indeed, but that was prior to our arrival and the facts we were able to ascertain. Armed with what we now know, there may be something yet to be learned from those occupants."

Thus we proceeded to the fourth floor, Holmes insisting that we take the stairs so as to investigate any clues that might have been left in the stairwell.

While I have led a somewhat adventurous life at Holmes' side, my days as a school athlete and soldiers' medic in Her Majesty's service were long behind me and I must admit to a fatigue and shortness of breath upon reaching our destination.

I was thus attempting to restore my normal breathing pattern when Holmes knocked upon the first door of his enquiries.

It was opened by young man, likely in his late-twenties, just under six feet in height, with dark brown hair and eyes, and an athletic build.

At first he appeared startled to see us, but then I realized that he must have been reacting to my wheezy condition, for I had bent over slightly to facilitate my oxygen intake.

"May I … oh, sir, please come in and sit down. Shall I call for a doctor?"

"No, no thank you young man," I replied, gratefully taking the proffered chair. "Just need to catch my breath. I'll be quite all right in a moment."

"Here, let me fetch you some brandy." As he strode to the sideboard to pour a glass of the ever popular stimulant, Holmes introduced us.

"Thank you, sir," he interjected. "My name is Sherlock Holmes and this is my colleague, Dr. Watson. I'm afraid I miscalculated the effort required to ascend the stairs to this level. Are you quite all right, Doctor?"

I nodded in the affirmative as I took the elixir offered by our host.

"Sherlock Holmes?" the man repeated, then looked at me. "Then you must be Dr. John Watson, the author. I've read some of your works. Are you sure your leg is all right? My own father also suffered a wound, in Her Majesty's Service, that left his leg damaged, and stairs are very bothersome to him."

I assured the fellow that I was fine and thanked him for his concern and the drink.

"I imagine that you are here regarding the break-in at Mr. Clemens' room down the hall," he remarked to my companion.

"Indeed," Holmes answered. "I believe you are the Honourable Ward James, of Bristol, son of the Earl of Roseboro?"

"I am, sir", he replied. "You must have spoken to Inspector Hopkins. He was here yesterday. May I offer you a drink, Mr. Holmes?"

He had poured one for himself and gestured an empty glass toward my companion

"Thank you, no. I understand that you were here in your rooms on the night in question?"

"Only to sleep, Mr. Holmes," he answered, taking a sip of his own brandy. "Inspector Hopkins said the incident took place on Thursday night. I left that evening at seven and returned close to midnight."

"May I enquire as to your activities that evening?"

"Well, I don't see how that will help, but I was picked up here by Mr. Harold Reese to meet with Sir Edwin Snider. Harry's an old school chum and a solicitor with the firm of Davis, Davis and Howard. He acts as our legal advisor here in London. We had dinner at Rivano's and discussed some financial matters with Sir Edwin, wherein I was representing my father. Then Harry and I dropped Sir Edwin at the Diogenes Club. We went on to the Sanford House to play billiards until eleven, when we called it a night and I returned here."

"And you saw nothing unusual or no one in the hallway upon your return?"

"As I told Inspector Hopkins, all was quiet and the hallway quite empty when I arrived."

Holmes digested that statement, then, held out his hand to shake that of young James. "Thank you. I think that will be all I need for now. Will you be in town for long?"

"I'm meeting with some friends tomorrow at St. Paul's for church services and spending the afternoon with them. I'll be returning to Bristol on Monday."

"Well then, enjoy your stay. Watson, are you quite recovered? Excellent! Let us be off to see the other guests. Good day, Mr. James."

After we exited and strode down the hall I queried my friend, "Any impressions, Holmes?"

"I'll not eliminate him as a suspect until I can confirm his alibi, Watson. I can tell you he is an excellent horseman, as he is, or has recently been, a frequent polo player. Also that billiards is a far less frequent pursuit."

"Yes, when he handed me my drink I noticed the blister between his left thumb and index finger where a billiard cue had rubbed it excessively. How did you arrive at polo?"

"Very good, Watson. The polo was also derived from his left hand and the toughness of the skin on the palm where one holds his reins, as well as the right hand where the pattern of callouses conforms to that of the polo mallet. Only an expert horseman can control his mount and strike a ball simultaneously."

Our next stop was the room directly across from Clemens' suite. This door was open by a gentleman of roughly fifty years of age, approximately six feet three inches in height with a barrel chest. His blue eyes were surrounded by lines that indicated much outdoor exposure to the sun, as was further evidenced by his tanned and leathered skin. His long brown hair was greying at the temples and his moustache was almost completely grey. His accent revealed that he also was American. He was in shirtsleeves with no collar or tie. His black trousers were held up by braces, and on his feet were black boots.

"Good afternoon. Mr. Hodges, I believe?"

"Yes, who are you?" He asked with a wary expression.

"My name is Sherlock Holmes and this is my colleague, Dr. Watson. We have been engaged by Scotland Yard to look into the matter of the burglary across the hall."

"Inspector Hopkins has already been here. I've told him all I know, which was nothing."

"I understand, Mr. Hodges," my friend replied, "but more facts have come to light that may be of importance. May we come in?"

The man hesitated and several seconds clicked by before he finally acquiesced.

"Very well," he finally stated, and stepped behind the door as he opened it to receive us.

After we had entered the room, Holmes and I turned back toward our host and found ourselves facing a .45 calibre Colt revolver.

Chapter Six

"I don't know what your game is, boys, but we do get the *real* Dr. Watson's reports in America, so I know that Sherlock Holmes died years ago. Now sit down over on that sofa and don't move."

With a heavy sigh Holmes sank into the sofa and I followed. My friend then declared, "Mr. Hodges, if you will be so kind as to call the manager's office I am sure we can clear this up, as I am obviously not deceased. I have merely requested my colleague not to write any more stories since my adventure at the Reichenbach Falls."

"Well, you just sit right there and we'll see about that." He then retreated out the door and across the hall, still keeping his pistol leveled at us through the open doorway. He knocked on Clemens' door and the aged author answered.

"Hello, Sam," our captor greeted. "I've got a couple birds here claiming to be Sherlock Holmes and Dr. Watson. Would you call down to the desk and have them send for the police?"

Looking beyond Hodges, Clemens gasped in astonishment. He reached out and pushed the man's outstretched gun hand down and exclaimed, "For god's sake, Gilbert, put down that Peacemaker! That *is* Sherlock Holmes and Dr. Watson. I met them at Baker Street just this morning and they're helping Scotland Yard with my burglary."

Thus admonished, the gentleman lowered his weapon. "Are you sure, Sam? What about that story of Holmes going over the waterfall with Moriarty?"

"I am not privy to the circumstances," replied Clemens, "but obviously our friend, Holmes here, survived that encounter."

He then came into the room to join us, with Hodges at his heels.

"My apologies gentlemen," the big man stated, returning his pistol to a holster on the coat rack behind the door, "but with Sam's burglary, I wasn't about to take any chances."

"Quite understandable, Mr. Hodges," my friend answered.

"And quite avoidable, Mr. Holmes," the elder American interjected, "if you would permit Watson here to continue his publishing of your adventures so that folks knew you survived Reichenbach. Why, come to think of it, I'd gladly pay for the privilege of publishing that story myself! My niece's husband, Charlie Webster and I own a publishing company you know. We did President Grant's autobiography a few years back."

"Now hold on just a minute, Sam," our gun-wielding host countered, "This sounds more like a magazine article than one of your books."

Turning his full attention to us, Hodges continued, "I represent *Century Magazine* gentlemen and, if you're of a mind, I could make you a generous offer for the story of what really happened at those Falls."

Holmes cut off these negotiations with a curt wave off of his hands in front of his face. "Gentlemen, I prefer not to discuss it. The matter at hand is the retrieval of Mr. Clemens' papers. That is my sole purpose at the moment. Now, if I may proceed?"

Reluctantly, the rival would-be publishers ceased and Clemens returned to his room after obtaining the promise of an update from Holmes as soon as possible.

Hodges, having seated himself in an armchair, offered us each a cigar in apology. Holmes accepted graciously. I hesitated, fearing that Hodges taste in cigars might be akin to Clemens', but then I noted that it was a familiar brand and gladly retrieved one for myself.

"So, Mr. Hodges," began my friend, after his first puff of smoke cleared his lips, "what brings a representative of *Century Magazine* to London?"

"Actually, Mr. Holmes," our host mumbled around his own cigar as he lit it, "I am on my way to Paris to get some background stories for the upcoming World Exhibition and Olympic Games. London is just a stopover."

"You seem a little off your regular beat, Mr. Hodges. Your accent is of the American Midwest, near Chicago, I would venture. I also perceive, by your leathered skin, ambling gait and the Stetson hat upon your coat rack, that you have spent considerable time in the American West, especially in the outdoors and on horseback. Your bearing suggests extensive exposure to military men at some point in your life. Your weapon and its unique holster suggest that the tamer life of civilized metropolises has not long been a common venue for your talents."

At this I noticed the holster and pistol hanging by the door. The holster was unique to my experience and I asked Hodges if I might take a closer look. He walked over and pulled the rig from the wall and handed it to me

The weapon itself was a Colt single action army revolver with ebony handles. The holster was a combination of straps much like a backpack, with the actual holster hanging down the left side where it would be concealed by the wearer's coat.

"How comfortable is this to wear, Mr. Hodges?" I enquired.

"Go ahead and try it on, Doctor," he replied.

I took off my coat and slipped my arms through the straps, and though he was a larger man than I, my impression was that a proper fit would be quite comfortable.

"Wherever did you get such a device?" I asked, handing the rig back to him and donning my coat again.

"Mr. Holmes is quite right about my past, Doctor," he answered, hanging the gun back up. "I was born in Chicago, went to Illinois State Normal University and apprenticed with the Chicago Tribune. In 1874 I was assigned to cover the Black Hills Gold Rush in the Dakotas and spent two years reporting stories of western lore and the exploits of the 7th cavalry under Colonel Custer."

"I thought Custer was a General," I interjected.

At this juncture Holmes interceded, "I believe, Custer's rank of General was a temporary promotion during the American Civil War and that was over a command of volunteers. He was reduced in rank when he was assigned to the regular army after the war ended."

"That's right, Mr. Holmes," replied Hodges. "You know our history."

"Individuals of certain types are always of interest to me, Mr. Hodges. Pray, continue your fascinating account."

I was somewhat surprised by this encouragement at story-telling from Holmes, who usually prefers to cut to the chase, but engrossed as I was, I was glad for it.

"Well, sir," Hodges responded through a cloud of smoke from his cigar. "That led me to be the reporter on site at Fort Lincoln when the news of the massacre of Custer's troops arrived in July of '76. I was still doing follow up stories when I happened to be in Deadwood on August 2 and witnessed the assassination of Wild Bill Hickok by Jack McCall. Now

Hickok's hardware would have fascinated you, Doctor Watson. His favorite guns were a pair of cap-and-ball Colt Navy pistols with ivory handles, silver plating and engraved with his name. He wore his revolvers backwards in his sash, and hardy ever used holsters. He would draw using a reverse, twist like a cavalryman.

"Anyway, that story and the subsequent reporting on Jack McCall's trial, as well as the Custer coverage, cemented my reputation at the Tribune and they pretty much gave me carte blanche to roam the West and file stories as I found them on a regular basis. I met Wyatt Earp late in '76 in Deadwood and followed his career, as well as Bat Masterson and some others, especially in Dodge City, Kansas. There was a wild place I tell you. Then I found myself down in Tombstone, Arizona with the Earp brothers and was there during the shootout at the O.K. Corral in '81. By the way, Marshal Earp did not use any so-called "Buntline Special" at that gun battle. He carried an 8 inch barrelled Smith and Wesson .44.

"Now all this time out West had convinced me of the necessity of carrying a pistol, which I wore on my hip in the standard fashion. But as I witnessed that gunplay from across the street, a wild shot grazed my hat and I spent that evening doing a lot of soul-searching about my career choice and how close I had come to meeting my Maker.

"I made up my mind then and there to pursue stories of a less violent nature and soon left town in the company of the vaudevillian, Eddie Foy, to try covering the theatre circuit.

"Eventually my writing kept me more in the larger cities where open and obvious gun display was frowned upon, so I had an old saddler friend of mine make up that rig for me. I use the ebony handles to keep everything on the dark side so it won't show so obvious inside my coat. I joined Century publishing a couple years later and moved back East, where I still cover many outdoor events such as circuses, baseball games and horseracing, but I always carry my trusty Colt when I'm in a strange town, at least until I get the lay of the land.

"But here I am, ramblin' along like some barfly hopin' for a drink to reward his tales. You say you have questions, Mr. Holmes?"

Holmes blew a ring of smoke into the air and answered, "I am told, by Inspector Hopkins, that you had an early dinner and were back here in your rooms by seven-thirty."

"Yes, that's correct."

"And that you heard nothing unusual and had no occasion to look out into the hallway and see anyone suspicious."

"Correct again, Mr. Holmes."

"Then I have only one question for you, sir. Did you put your boots out in the hall for the porter to shine and, if so, what time did you do so?"

Chapter Seven

"My boots?" repeated our host.

"If you would indulge me, please," responded Holmes.

"Well, let me think," Hodges replied, cocking his head to one side, as if that would help focus the picture in his mind's eye.

"I wore my black dress shoes to dinner, so that night I had put my brown boots out for a clean and polish at six when I left. They had not yet been picked up when I returned at seven-thirty."

"Yes," said the detective. "The hotel shoe service is usually a late night endeavour and the shoes are returned by dawn the next morning. May I see them, please?"

With a look of wonderment and a shake of his shaggy head, the big American strolled back to his bedroom and returned with a large pair of Western style boots which he handed to Holmes.

My friend then went into his examination with gusto. He held the sole of the left boot level to his eye and peered along its not inconsiderable length. He pulled his tape measure from one pocket to verify width and size and then exchanged his tape for his magnifying glass which he used to examine the sole in depth, especially around the stitching. Satisfied he returned the boot with a nod.

"Thank you, Mr. Hodges. We shall not take up any more of your time. Come, Watson, we've other guests to query."

Holmes stood and started for the door. Hodges spluttered "Mr. Holmes, what is it? What's so important about my left boot?"

"A trivial matter, Mr. Hodges," said Holmes with a wave. "Thank you for your fine cigar and the fascinating stories of your career."

I followed Holmes, shaking the perplexed Hodges by the hand, at which point he recovered and stated, "Remember my offer, Dr. Watson. We'll pay you well for the story of Holmes' survival, or any other adventures you've not yet published."

I nodded and non-committedly stated "Thank you, sir. I will keep it in mind."

Catching up to Holmes in the hall I also queried him about the boot.

"It doesn't prove anything, Watson," he replied, "but it is the size and shape of the footprints we found in Clemens room."

"So Hodges could be our thief?" I asked.

"Too soon for that, my friend," he answered. "It could have been him in that room, or it could have been someone who borrowed his boots from the hallway unobserved and used them to plant a false clue."

"It seems to me that this planting of false clues is as much a mystery as the theft itself." I observed.

"Excellent, Watson! And it may well prove our prey's downfall. Had he, or they, simply done a smash and grab of several valuables, our list of suspects would be innumerable. But this, this is too precise. Ah, here we are." He stated, stopping at the next room on his list. "This would be Mr. and Mrs. J. R. Robinson. They arrived on Thursday afternoon."

The Robinsons proved to be a young couple purportedly on their honeymoon. He was in his mid-twenties, she looked only to be eighteen or nineteen. The groom was a lean five foot eight inches in height with sandy hair and blue eyes. His occupation was as an apprentice draftsman to the architectural firm of Larker and Moon in Manchester. His wife, a petite brunette with soft brown eyes and a shy smile, was the former Rachel Larker, daughter of one of the partners.

Having introduced ourselves we were invited in by the excitable young man.

"Please come in, sirs," he exclaimed. Turning to his wife who had just come in from the dressing room he said,

"Rachel, this is Mr. Sherlock Holmes and Dr. Watson! Can you believe it?"

Bowing her head in a curtsey she responded animatedly, "Oh my goodness! Please, gentlemen, sit down. Can I get you anything? We still have some tea." She went for the pot but discovered it no longer warm. "Oh dear, I'm afraid it has cooled too much. I can ring down for more ..."

Holmes raised a hand, "Please do not trouble yourself, Mrs. Robinson, our stay will be brief. I've only a few questions regarding the events of Thursday evening."

At that she froze and stared at her husband who cleared his throat, "Ah, gentlemen, I don't wish to be rude but what business are our, ah, honeymoon activities to you?"

Holmes arched his eyebrow and I, realizing the young man's apprehension, broke in to explain.

"Mr. Robinson, we are here regarding the burglary down the hall in Mr. Clemens' suite. We only wish to know anything you might have seen or heard."

His young wife began to breathe again and lowered herself down on the settee next to her groom, instinctively wrapping her arm around his.

"Oh," he replied, his embarrassment coloring his cheeks. "I'm afraid we don't know anything about that. Thursday evening you say?"

I replied in the affirmative while Holmes consulted his notes.

"Ah, I see that Inspector Hopkins was not able to interview you earlier," stated my friend. "Yes, the American author, Samuel Clemens, down in Room 404, was burgled while he and his family were out Thursday, sometime between 6:00 p.m. and midnight."

"Oh, my goodness!" exclaimed the young bride, clutching the collar of her dress to her throat. "Burglars!"

Robinson, putting on his best new husband bravado, patted her arm and told her, "There's no need to fear, my Sweet. No thief would attempt to burgle an occupied room in the middle of London, especially up here on the fourth floor."

Turning to Holmes, he raised his own eyebrows, as if to draw out a confirmation of his statement for his wife's benefit.

Holmes rose to the occasion and affirmed the young man's conclusion. "Your husband is correct, Mrs. Robinson. Even this attempt was made only because the thief was after something very specific and valuable and knew exactly when the Clemens family would be out."

"But, surely hotel security should be better than that?" She cried, looking at her wedding ring, a thin band of gold that, while not terribly expensive, was probably worth more than the treasure of Agra to her.

"That is one of the reasons for our investigation, madam," Holmes continued, putting her at ease, "to ensure that no such thing occurs again. Now, did either of you have occasion to see or hear anything out in the hallway during the hours I mentioned?"

Receiving a negative response, as they had ordered room service for dinner and, we could obviously infer, were otherwise occupied, we excused ourselves and proceeded on to the next tenant.

This, I was pleasantly surprised to learn, was Adelaide Savage who, with her children, occupied the room across from the Robinsons and next door to Clemens.

The door was opened to Holmes' knock by George, whose face broke into a broad smile when he saw us.

"Good afternoon, Mr. Holmes. Hello, Dr. Watson, please come in."

He retreated into the room and led us to some easy chairs while he called out to his mother.

Adelaide glided into the room with an excited air and we immediately rose to greet her.

"Mr. Holmes, it is so good to see you," she smiled, taking his hand. "John, I hadn't expected to see again so soon." Her smile, if possible, seemed to beam brighter as she took my hand in both of hers.

"Please, gentlemen, sit down." We did so and I announced our purpose.

"It seems, Adelaide, that in all our catching up this morning I neglected to discover your proximity to our case. We are looking into the burglary of Mr. Clemens' room, just next door."

"Oh yes, Inspector Hopkins spoke with us about that. Is there something more you need to know?"

Holmes spoke out at that point, "Some further information has come to light, Mrs. Savage. I understand from Hopkins that none of you were aware of anything happening out on the fire escape, since your own curtains were closed against the chill of the evening. However, I do need to know if any of you saw anyone or anything out in the hallway that seemed unusual, no matter how trivial."

"Well," she answered, "we were supposed to leave for dinner at six but it was closer to twenty after by the time we departed."

George huffed, "Marina," he stated softly, obviously inferring that his sister's ablutions were the cause for their delayed departure.

His mother gave him a look and continued. "The only person in the hall was a waiter who had just delivered room service for someone. He rode down the lift with us."

Holmes leaned forward, "Could you describe him, please?"

"Oh, just an ordinary fellow," she replied. "He was young, in his twenties, with dark hair and clean shaven. I'm afraid that's all I can recall."

At this George spoke up, "He was about five foot nine, Mr. Holmes, and thin. He couldn't have weighed any more than I. He *was* clean-shaven but his sideburns were a bit long. They extended about an inch below the bottom of his ears, and his hair was parted on the right."

Holmes noted this information and responded, "You are very observant, young man."

"Well, he insisted that we get into the lift first and then he stepped in with his cart. With the four of us, plus the operator, it was quite full and not much to look at for a ride of five flights. I was just behind and to the right of him so those details were in my face the whole trip."

"Still I applaud your memory, George."

"One other thing, Mr. Holmes, I don't know if it is important, but it seemed unusual."

"The unusual is always worth noting," replied the detective.

"Yes, sir, it was when we stepped out into the hall. I saw a pair of brown boots outside the door across from Mr. Clemens'. Mother tells me that it is common for guests to put their boots out to be cleaned, but these seemed to be of an unusual style. I would have looked at them closer but we were running late already."

I responded to this observation myself. "Those were the boots of the American in Room 405, Mr. Hodges. They are a western American style so I'm not surprised they stood out to you."

"Oh, well that's not much of a help then." he replied solemnly.

"On the contrary," replied Holmes, "the timing of your observation is most helpful."

"Really?" the college-bound lad responded, his face brightening.

"Yes, indeed," answered Holmes. "I believe that will do for now. Thank you both," he said rising to leave.

"It is always a pleasure to see you, Mr. Holmes," Adelaide stated, taking his hand once again.

I also arose and, again, she took my hand in hers, "and don't you forget your promise, John, as soon as you are able."

"Indeed not, Adelaide," I responded, once more brushing the back of her hand with a gentle kiss.

Joining Holmes in the hallway I queried my friend, "Where to now?"

"That, Doctor, is the limit of our queries of the guests. The other rooms were either unoccupied or the residents have moved on in their travels. I shall follow up on some of those, meanwhile the night shift should have arrived by now. Let us return to Drysdale's office and arrange those interviews."

Chapter Eight

We again began a round of meetings with the hotel staff, all of whom were on duty on the night in question. None of the maids had been called into service on the fourth floor, the changing of linen and towels usually being done during the day. We did confirm that a young man, fitting George's description of him, delivered room service to the Robinsons at quarter past six. He did indeed, ride down the lift with the Savage family at six-twenty.

The bootblack reported that he did not pick up the shoes on the fourth floor until after one in the morning. He confirmed that Mr. Hodges brown western boots were among those he polished that night.

"Were the boots damp at all?" enquired Holmes.

"As a matter of fact they were, Mr. Holmes. That is, the soles had a couple of damp spots on them, like they had been completely wet earlier but were almost dry when I got to them. The uppers were quite dry. I thought that was a bit odd, myself. If the person wearing them had been out in the rain, I should have thought it more likely that the uppers would have been wet while the person would have dried off the bottom of their feet on the rug at the hotel entrance."

Holmes made note of that fact and we proceeded with our questioning.

All in all, none of the staff saw or heard anything that might assist our investigation. Having finished this task we adjourned to the lobby. Suddenly Holmes pulled me behind a pillar and bade me to be quiet.

"Watson, that man at the front desk, do you recognize him?"

I cautiously peeked around the pillar and saw a short, stout man of about 40 years sporting a light brown handlebar moustache. He was dressed for an evening out with his black topcoat draped over formal attire and a white scarf at his neck. His top hat was tilted to his left and there seemed to be an unusual reflection off his forehead.

Drawing back I spoke softly to my friend, "I see him, Holmes, what is your concern?"

"Think back to the case you chronicled as *The Red-Headed League*, Watson. Does he not seem familiar to you?"

Not wanting to seem overly observant of this individual, I leaned against the pillar, just beyond its edge, and lit a cigarette. Appearing to be engaged in this activity I stole a look at the gentleman again. He turned in my direction as I did so, but did not appear to notice me as he continued to move around toward the hotel entrance. From this new angle I espied that the reflection on his forehead was really an apparent mark left by a splash of acid.

I turned back to Holmes, "Could that have been John Clay?" Noting my use of the past tense Holmes quickly stepped around me and saw his quarry leaving, "Watson, learn what you can about him from the desk clerk, I'll meet you back at Baker Street." He quickly moved after the gentleman and disappeared into the darkness outside.

I watched in wonder and then proceeded to the desk to enquire after this mysterious guest. Craig, the desk clerk, advised me that the gentleman was, indeed, John Clay, Duke of Dartford, and that he had been a guest in Room 304 for a week. He was due to depart on Wednesday.

For those readers who may be unfamiliar with this person, it was October of 1890, when Holmes was called upon by Mr. Jabez Wilson, a pawnbroker, who was upset over the loss of a part-time situation he had obtained through a fraudulent organization called The Red Headed League. After several weeks work, he arrived at his job one day to find a note stating the League dissolved and he out of an easy £4 per week.

Holmes discerned that Wilson's new assistant, Vincent Spaulding, an alias being used by John Clay, had conspired with others to set up the phony League. He was using his employer's time away from the shop to descend into the basement, where he had ostensibly set up a photography studio. In actuality he was tunnelling through to the Coburg Branch of the City and Suburban Bank where an unusually large shipment of French Gold was on hand in the underground vault.

Holmes foiled the plot and Clay was arrested by Inspector Jones of Scotland Yard. At the time Jones described him to Bank Director Merryweather thusly:

'John Clay, the murderer, thief, smasher, and forger. He's a young man, Mr. Merryweather, but he is at the head of his profession, and I would rather have my bracelets on him than on any criminal in London. He's a remarkable man, is young John Clay. His grandfather was a royal duke, and he himself has been to Eton and Oxford. His brain is as cunning as his fingers, and though we meet signs of him at every turn, we never know where to find the man himself. He'll crack a crib in Scotland one week, and be raising money to build an orphanage in Cornwall the next.'

Having confirmed Clay's identity with Craig, I exited the hotel and found a cab for my return to Baker Street. The temperature had continued its fall with the setting of the sun. Small snowflakes began descending through the dark night and into the glow of the streetlamps.

Twenty minutes later, I was ensconced in front of the fire that Mrs. Hudson had kept kindled in our sitting room.

It was now nearly seven o'clock and Mrs. Hudson enquired about dinner. I informed her that I had no idea when Holmes might be returning.

"Well, I can keep it hot until seven-thirty, Doctor, after that it'll burn to a crisp."

"Can it be turned off now and reheated when Holmes returns?" I asked.

She folded her arms, spoon in hand, and gave me a withering look. "In all my years of cooking for that man, I should know better. I'll do it, Dr. Watson, but I'll not take responsibility for the quality and I'd better not hear one word of complaint!"

"You have the patience of Job, Mrs. Hudson, and I thank you for your forbearance."

By 8:00 p.m., Holmes had still not arrived and so I requested my own dinner from our long suffering landlady. She brought my portion forth and informed me that she would wrap the rest and put it in the icebox if Holmes should ever decide to return.

It was well that she did so, for it was quarter past midnight before my detective friend finally returned.

As he threw off his hat and coat I informed him that his dinner was downstairs to which he waved off my statement and instead, loaded his Meerschaum pipe with a pleasant cherry blend of tobacco.

I then told Holmes that the desk clerk had identified Clay as the Duke of Dartford.

He raised his eyebrows at me and answered, "Clay's claim to that title is entirely false, Watson. While his paternal grandfather did indeed hold that rank, it died out with him, as having no legitimate male heirs. Clay's father was the result of a liaison between the Duke and a Gypsy maiden. This Gypsy background is the reason for Clay's pierced ears, by the way."

He took a long draw from his pipe and then asked, "How long has Clay been registered at the Langham and where is his room?"

I replied "He has been there a week and is scheduled to leave on Wednesday. More telling is that his suite is 304, right below Clemens."

This news was met by a narrowing of Holmes gaze and then a closing of his eyes in thought. After a minute he opened them again and spoke, "Watson, you must be exhausted. I insist that you be off to bed while I think this through. I shall avail myself of a cold supper from Mrs. Hudson's kitchen and smoke another pipe or two."

"But, what of your evening, Holmes?" I demanded, "Where did Clay go? Did he meet anyone? Is he involved in our case?"

Standing, Holmes made his way toward the door and the promising kitchen below. "All in good time, Watson. Let us continue this discussion in the morning after a night's rest. Perhaps Morpheus will give us a new perspective."

His disappearance out the door left me no choice but to acquiesce to his wishes. Thus, I took myself off to bed, vowing to get my answers at breakfast.

Chapter Nine

Breakfast, however, showed no sign of Holmes. Although I had arisen at eight o'clock, I was informed by Mrs. Hudson that I had missed his departure by half an hour. He had left a note for me to wait for answers to two telegrams he had sent the previous evening and to bring them to him at the Langham Hotel where he would be gathering more information from Clemens.

One of those answers arrived as I was reading his note. In the meantime, Mrs. Hudson served up some scones and coffee and I prepared myself for a new day of chronicling my friend's latest case.

It was nine-thirty before the second reply to Holmes' enquiries arrived. I immediately set off for the Langham with these missives in hand.

There was a fair amount of snow on the ground and it was still lightly falling, but the streets were passable and my cab made good time. I checked with the day clerk on the desk and ascertained that Holmes was still upstairs with Clemens. I made my way to the lift forthwith.

My knock on Clemens' door was met by his daughter, Jean. She was a charming young lady of twenty years with auburn hair, a trim figure and expressive eyes. She escorted me to the study where her father and Holmes were engaged in conversation.

"Ah, Watson, there you are! Have you my answers?"

I reached into my pocket, withdrew the telegrams and placed them into his hands. I sat down at the table where he and Clemens had apparently shared coffee.

"Might I offer you some coffee, Doctor?" asked Jean in her pleasant voice. I accepted gladly as Holmes pored over the telegraph forms.

Clemens, himself, turned to me and asked, "Would you care for a cigar, Doctor?" as he reached for a tin on the table.

Dreading even a whiff of his tobacco I instead offered him one of my own with an encouragement to 'Try one of our English cigars'. Fortunately for my sinuses, he accepted and soon a pleasant aroma wafted about the room. The bright glow of the end of my cigar seemed to attract General Grant and I again found the feline in my lap.

"Well," exclaimed the author of Tom Sawyer, "it seems the General has taken a liking to you, Dr. Watson."

"I thought he was afraid of fire," I said, stroking his back with my free hand.

"Well, to be technical," answered Clemens "he's afraid of flames, such as the lighting of a match. The glow of a cigar or cigarette, don't seem to bother him none."

"Speaking of General Grant," interjected Holmes, as he stuffed the telegrams into his inner coat pocket, "I take it there was some rivalry between yourself and Mr. Hodges' employers over the publication of the former president's autobiography?"

"Now I don't know that 'rivalry' would be the correct phrase, Mr. Holmes," stated Clemens in his slow drawl. "You see, Century Publishing is a magazine publisher. I, myself, advertise my works in their pages. They persuaded the General to write some articles for them about his Civil War experiences, the various battles and so forth. At this point in his life Ulysses was in financial straits and he was happy to accept the five hundred dollars per article that Century offered him. The thing which astounded me was that, as admirable a man as Richard Gilder, the Editor in Chief certainly is, and with a heart which is in the right place, it had never seemed to occur to him that to offer General Grant five hundred dollars for a magazine article was not only the monumental injustice of the nineteenth century, but of all centuries. He ought to have known that if he had given General Grant a check for ten thousand dollars, the sum would still have been trivial; that if he had paid him twenty thousand dollars for a single article, the sum would still have been inadequate; that if he had paid him thirty thousand dollars for a single magazine war article, it still could not be called paid for; that if he had given him forty thousand dollars for a single magazine article, he would still be in General Grant's debt.

"When I discovered what was going on and that the General was thinking about putting all his stories into a book about his life, I hightailed down to his place in New Jersey and offered my advice to make sure he was treated fair."

"So this is how you came to be Grant's book publisher," stated Holmes, obviously hoping to stave off any further storytelling by the master American storyteller. "Were there any hard feelings on the part of Century, in that you had purloined their source of increased circulation?"

Clemens paused over that question for a moment then replied, "I don't believe so, Mr. Holmes. I'm sure they recognized their lack of experience in book publishing. My god, they were going to pay the General a 10% royalty on projected sales of 25,000 and only work with bookstores. My nephew and I put together a subscription network that sold so many copies that Grant's widow, Julia, was eventually paid $450,000."

"That sounds like a motive for getting even," I chimed in.

"I hadn't really thought in those terms, Doctor. Obviously their method wouldn't have garnered anywhere near as much as mine, so's I don't see how they could compare the two."

"Still," intoned Holmes, "we shouldn't dismiss the possibility. How well do you know Mr. Hodges?"

"Gilbert? Oh, we've run into each other from time to time. He's a fair reporter and a pretty good writer. Once he's got a scent of a story he goes after it like a bulldog."

"And a bit trigger happy?" I questioned.

"Well ..." uttered Clemens, "I wouldn't go so far as to say that. He may be quick to pull his gun, but I've never known him to actually shoot someone. Leastways not since he came East and started working for Century."

"Let's pass on Hodges for the moment," said Holmes, reaching into his pocket and sliding a newspaper engraving across the table. "Have you had any encounters with this man within the last week? Keep in mind that this picture is nearly ten years old and that he now has a moustache."

I leaned over and saw that the likeness was that of John Clay from the time of his trial for his attempted bank robbery.

Clemens studied the picture as he puffed away at his cigar, holding it up so he might catch a better light on it. Handing it back to my friend he shook his head.

"No, I can't say for sure. I know I haven't met any such person formally, but he has a familiarity that I may have seen him in a crowd or passed by him somewheres. Is that white mark on his forehead a permanent fixture or was that just an error in the printing process?"

Holmes tucked the clipping away and answered, "Oh, the mark is quite permanent, I assure you, an accident of his youth that resulted in a splash of acid that blanched his skin."

"How is he related to the case?" Clemens asked.

"He may not be," responded Holmes. "However, for now he is a person of interest that I must investigate to ascertain his status. In fact," Holmes continued, noting the time, "I should be moving on to that point of enquiry right now. If you will excuse us, sir?"

Clemens stood with us and bid us good luck as we exited his suite. Once in the hallway I enquired after the replies to Holmes' telegrams and his actions of the previous evening.

"The British penal system is in utter disarray, Watson!" Holmes exclaimed. "Clay is not an escaped prisoner but has recently been paroled, one year before his 10 year sentence was to conclude."

"Impossible!" I replied, "Did not Inspector Jones charge him with murder, as well as forgery and attempted bank robbery?"

"I recall that statement made by the good Inspector, Watson. However, he had no proof for his allegations, so Clay was only convicted upon the bank robbery attempt which we interrupted.

"Personally, I do not believe Clay to be a violent man. His forte was forgery and counterfeiting checks. His victims were always among the wealthy or banks or insurance companies. His pathological need being to take from those who were of a station in life that he felt he was denied because his bloodline was tainted. I also believe that his founding of the orphanage in Cornwall was an effort to help those, who like himself, were denied a legitimate childhood."

"Then what is he doing here? Where did he go last night?"

As we walked to the lift he replied, "Clay's sojourn merely took him to the theatre, Watson, where he enjoyed a concert of the Italian virtuoso violinist, Biagio Ricciardo, who is excellent, by the way. He remained for the entire performance. Then he removed himself to one of the finer gentlemen's clubs of the City. He met no one in particular at the theatre and merely settled in at his club for some refreshment. Some few members greeted him amicably as they passed by his table, but none sat to converse with him. He then returned to the Langham shortly before midnight."

"So, what is our next move then?" I asked.

As we entered the lift, Holmes looked at me and told the operator "Three," and we were soon walking down the hall toward Room 304.

"In case you were wondering, Holmes, I am not armed."

My friend replied, "I was aware of that, Watson. The lack of bulge of your coat packet revealed as much, but I am convinced that weapons will not be necessary for this meeting."

Holmes knocked on the former convict's door and it was answered promptly by a manservant. The young man was about my height, that is, about three inches short of six feet,[1] with dark curly hair, clean-shaven and built much like a boxer. His youth and physique classified him as someone I would not wish to tangle with.

Upon observing us with quick, piercing brown eyes, he enquired, "Yes, gentlemen?"

---

[1] Sir Arthur Conan Doyle never mentioned Watson's height. This measurement is based upon the height of Edward Hardwicke's portrayal of Watson in the Granada Television Series (1986-1994).

Holmes responded, "Please inform Mr. Clay that Sherlock Holmes and Dr. Watson request an audience with him."

"I will inform the Duke, sir. Please wait here." He closed the door on us and, I presume, went to inform his master.

Less than a minute later the door opened again and we were ushered into the sitting area by the young man.

"Please take a seat, gentlemen. The Duke will be with you momentarily."

"We will stand, if you please, thank you," answered Holmes.

Our wait was not long. Clay soon entered the room wearing a maroon smoking jacket, black trousers and highly polished black shoes with gleaming white spats.

Not surprisingly he did not offer us a handshake. He took a seat and waved us toward the settee. "Please, gentlemen, do sit down. I believe we have much to discuss and there is no reason why we shouldn't all be comfortable.

"Gilliam!" he called to his man. "Please bring some brandy, or would you prefer tea, Mr. Holmes?"

"Nothing for us, thank you," answered my friend, as we finally sat down. "We've just come from taking refreshment with Mr. Clemens."

At the mention of the American's name, Clay's face brightened.

"Ah the famous 'Mark Twain'. I have heard he was here at the Langham, but I have not had the pleasure of meeting him. As a matter of fact, I was planning on attending his lecture tonight at the Theatre Royal, Drury Lane."

Gilliam appeared with a small brandy for our host and then retreated to another room. I was sure, however, that he would materialize at a moment's notice should his master require it.

"I am sure you will find it thoroughly entertaining, John Clay," replied Holmes.

At the use of his familiar name, Clay's features darkened and he took a sip of his brandy. Then he appeared to relax and a smile spread over his features.

"There was a time, Mr. Sherlock Holmes, that I would have had you and Dr. Watson forcibly removed for your impudence. But my years as Her Majesty's guest have somewhat tempered my youthful ire. You know by all the rights of blood succession that I am the rightful Duke of Dartford."

"Believe it or not, sir, I do sympathize with your plight, if not your methods of dealing with it," answered the detective.

"Really?" questioned the pretender to royalty. "And you, Dr. Watson, are you in agreement, or is the slight scowl I perceive upon your face indicative of a more prejudicial opinion?"

Slightly flustered at having my emotion so easily read I cleared my throat and answered, "Holmes has explained the unfortunate circumstance of your father's birth, sir. But just as I recognize that you had no control over that, you must also reconcile yourself to the fact that you have no control over the rules of British peerage. Your actions of the past may have felt justified in your sight, but they cannot be condoned by law-abiding citizens."

Clay raised his eyes to the ceiling and pondered a moment then returned his gaze upon me with a glance at Holmes.

"And what do you know of my actions that you would condemn me? Would that be the orphanage I founded down in Cornwall? The funds I donated to hospitals to care for children of the poor? The scholarship I set up at Eton, which unfortunately ran out of funds and denied educational opportunities to a half dozen deserving boys while I was incarcerated? For what actions do you condemn me, Doctor?"

"From what I have heard, I, uh, would question the source of those funds." I stated, hesitantly.

"From what you have heard?" Clay repeated, "I would imagine the source of these stories to be highly questionable in themselves. I have read your account of the *Red Headed League*, Doctor, and, were he not retired, I would bring suit against that fool Inspector Jones for his slanderous statements."

Turning to my friend he continued, "What of you, Mr. Detective? Your reputation would indicate that you should have a knowledge of my situation which would make judgments of me less severe."

Holmes peered at the man and then sat back, crossing his legs and reaching into his breast pocket. "Do you mind if I smoke, sir?"

Clay nodded his ascent and Holmes lit up a cigarette very deliberately. Slowly exhaling a puff of smoke, he voiced the following narrative.

"What I know of you, as indisputable facts, are that you were born in 1860 to Stefan and Simza Clay and your birth name is Ion, which you changed when you went to school. Your father, in turn was the illegitimate son of George Clay, the Duke of Dartford, and your grandmother, Nadya."

At the mention of his grandmother's name, Clay exploded, "She was *talaitha,* a maiden, who was forced upon by that scoundrel, Dartford.

"But Gypsies get no justice against 'gentlemen' and she was denied acknowledgement of her resulting child."

Holmes held up his hand, "I was aware of that story. Having studied the Duke's history, I am inclined to believe it to be true, which is why I sympathize with your claim."

Clay took another sip of his brandy, "Thank you, Holmes."

Nodding his acknowledgement of Clay's appreciation my redoubtable friend continued. "As you approached your own youth, your father acquired the funds to send you to Eton and Oxford where you did quite well. While you were at Oxford, however, your parents were killed in a road accident.

"It was at this point that you became introduced to the mysterious benefactor who had supplied your father the funds for your schooling, one Professor James Moriarty."

Chapter Ten

"**M**oriarty!" I exclaimed.

"Yes, Doctor" my friend answered "and it was he who took the impressionable young Mr. Clay and twisted his talents and fed his thirst for revenge against the upper classes."

"Stop!" shouted Clay, suddenly standing before us with clenched fists. Gilliam came rushing in from the next room ready to protect or act on his master's behalf.

I stood quickly as well, in case the situation should turn violent. Holmes merely looked up at his host with, I daresay, pity on his face and remained in his seat.

Clay clenched and unclenched his fists and finally put a hand to his chest, as if to control his breathing and elevated heart rate.

Slowly he spoke again, "The professor took care of me. He gave me work and paid me well. It was through his generosity and advice on investments that I have been able to accumulate the funds for my charitable deeds. I should hate you for his death, Mr. Holmes, but Colonel Moran says he witnessed the act and could not prevent the Professor from his obsessive attack upon you, to which you reacted in self-defence."

Somewhat calmer, Clay continued, "My temper gets the better of me at times, sir. It has been a failing since childhood. Prison has not completely eliminated that disposition and I only have Gilliam here to thank for keeping me alive when my fits against other inmates may have resulted in disaster for myself."

He sat back down and so did I, as Gilliam stood back but did not leave the room.

"You are an artist of the first water," continued my friend, "I even have one of your paintings in my own abode, an excellent copy of *The Astronomer* by the Dutch painter, Gerrit Dou. I also suspect that there are many other 'masters' owned by London's upper classes, who thought they were obtaining the actual works from Moriarty, when in fact you were the artist in his employ."

"Really, Mr. Holmes you flatter me. If I had such talent I could sell my own works," responded our reluctant host.

"As indeed you should," answered Holmes, "It would prove most lucrative I'm sure. Certainly it will be less dangerous than when Moriarty seized upon that talent and used you to copy paintings, forge signatures on cheques, and create other legal documents that increased his own wealth and powerbase. The fact that, in some cases, you were forging the names of men recently dispatched by the Professor's minions is, I am sure, why Jones accused you of murder as well."

Clay grew impatient, "Surely, Mr. Holmes, you must have some purpose for coming here other than to discuss my life story. Have you a question for me?"

Holmes stared at the man and I could almost see his great brain whipping through a myriad of calculations in a mere moment, then he spoke.

"For now, I've only one. On Thursday evening the hotel staff indicates that you went out at four-thirty and returned at six-thirty."

"Yes, that is correct."

"And you, Gilliam, where were you during that time?"

"His Grace had no need of my services for that evening," the strapping young man answered. "I left at the same time and joined some old friends at the Cock's Crow for dinner. Some of us went on for a game of billiards and I returned here by eleven."

Holmes noted that and returned his questioning to Clay.

"On Thursday, sometime between six o'clock and midnight, Mr. Clemens' rooms were burgled and they happen to be right above yours."

Again Clay leaned forward and looked sharply at the detective, "Are you implying ..."

Holding up his hand Holmes retorted, "Calm yourself, I merely wish to know if you heard or saw anything out of the ordinary while you were here alone, especially anything outside on the fire escape."

Clay sat back and briefly closed his eyes with a hand to his forehead. After a few moments he looked up and answered.

"When I returned, I changed clothes and spent the evening reading in this very room. I heard nothing but the sound of the storm outside. I remember there were some thunder bursts that rattled the windows and shook the fire escape, but I paid little attention."

Holmes eyes brightened, "Do you remember what time that was?"

Clay shook his head, "No, Mr. Holmes, I had no reason to check the clock. I can only tell you it was earlier rather than later, certainly no later than eight o'clock."

"I see" he replied softly, then louder he posed, "One last thing I wish from you and then we shall take our leave. May I examine your fire escape?"

Clay nodded and waved him toward the balcony doors. Holmes stepped out and proceeded to use his glass to examine the rails from which he had to brush off the newly fallen snow. Afterward he returned to the warmth of Clay's suite.

"I am sorry to have disturbed you, gentlemen. Come, Watson, we've other enquiries to make. Mr. Clay," he hesitated, "for your charitable works I would wish that you were, 'Sir John', but for now know that I do not believe your attempt at the French gold was your idea. It is not where your talents lie. Your loyalty to Moriarty in not implicating his planning of the heist has cost you these past nine years. I hope your future will serve you better."

As we made for the door, Gilliam moved ahead and opened it. When we stepped through Holmes stopped and asked one final question, this addressed to the valet.

"Gilliam, where did you play your billiard games that night?"

The young man looked puzzled and answered, "We were at Sanfords, sir"

*****

"Holmes," I asked my friend as we again made for the lift, "do you believe his story?"

"Let us discuss it back at Baker Street," he replied, shifting his eyes towards the lift operator as the doors opened, indicating that he preferred a private discussion.

Forestalling that, I did ask him about his second telegram reply as we settled into the cab that would take us home.

"I was curious, Watson, about our honeymooners. The Langham is, after all, a grand hotel and not generally in the budget of someone in Mr. Robinson's position. I telegraphed Chief Constable Keyzers in Manchester to ascertain what information he could provide on our young couple.

"Apparently, Robinson obtained a personal leave of absence from his employer to attend to 'family business', in London before his upcoming nuptials. The next day, Miss Larker's parents found her gone also, leaving a note stating she was eloping with her young man."

Dismayed, I responded, "That will not bode well for them at all, Holmes. He may well find himself out of a job for such actions and then where will they be?"

"I will leave matters of the heart to you, Doctor" Holmes replied. "My only concern is their relation to our case. If Robinson needs money he has a motive to be our thief but, unless he is far more clever than I perceive, he will remain at the bottom of our suspect pool."

Arriving at our lodgings Holmes paid the cabbie and we dashed through the falling snow into the warmth of Mrs. Hudson's abode. As dutiful as ever she had kept the fire in our rooms well stoked and we doffed our hats and overcoats to sit by its warmth. She poked her head in to enquire about our desire for lunch and we answered in the affirmative.

Stuffing his pipe with shag, Holmes settled into his chair. I pulled my notes from my pocket and began re-writing some notations that I had hastily scribbled which were nearly illegible. I knew that Holmes would speak in his own good time and I did not press him as to his thoughts just yet. We continued in these silent activities until our lunch arrived. When we sat at our table to partake Mrs. Hudson's culinary efforts, Holmes finally spoke.

"John Clay presents an interesting conundrum," he began. "I have no doubt that he, with the young Mr. Gilliam as his accomplice, could have pulled off the Clemens' heist quite easily. On the other hand, so could Mr. James in concert with his friend Reese. Hodges with an as yet unknown partner. Robinson and his wife could have done the deed as well. None of them have perfect alibis. Even the Savages could have physically accomplished the feat.

At this I bristled, "Surely not, Holmes! How could you even suspect ..."

But he waved me silent with his fork in hand, "I do not suspect them, Watson, I merely state that, to someone who does not know them as we do, they could physically have worked in tandem to do the deed and then been each other's alibi. The young man, were he so inclined and skilled, could have performed the theft and lowered the papers to his mother and sister in the alley below. Who would suspect a mother and daughter, out walking with their shopping bags, to be in possession of the stolen works of a great American author?"

Grudgingly I conceded his point, "As you say, Holmes, if they were a family of thieves, but since we know better, I would be more inclined toward Clay and Gilliam."

Holmes took a healthy swallow of his tea and looked to the ceiling, shaking his head. "I need more data, Watson! More to the point, we need motive. What could any of *these* people want with Clemens' papers?"

"Again, I would lean toward Clay," I suggested. "Once in possession of Clemens' papers he could use his forgery skills in all manner of ways to make money off of them."

"A possibility, Watson," Holmes conceded, "but I need to make more enquiries into all the possible players in this game."

He tossed his napkin down on his plate and strode off to his room. I finished my meal as well and pondered over a cigarette as I watched the weather turn from our consulting room window. The clouds had grown darker and the snow was falling heavier. There was only a light breeze, thus the flakes were dropping nearly straight down and beginning to pile into drifts. Traffic on the street had nearly dissipated as cabbies made for their stables to wait out the storm.

The creature who soon emerged from Holmes' room bore little resemblance to my housemate. A salt and pepper beard and moustache spread across his lower face and a shabby brown overcoat, splotched with stains and some few tears encased his figure. He did not reduce his stature, as he so often did when incognito, and I put this down as a concession to the cold which would take its toll on muscles in a prolonged contorted position. A java brown, short-crowned hat with a wide brim settled upon his head, wherein he had brushed in some grey to his hair. Round, tortoise shell framed eyeglasses rested upon his nose.

The entire effect made his usually long angular face appear much rounder and not at all like the aquiline features of my famous friend.

"Holmes," I expressed with some concern, "surely you are not venturing out in this weather now? The snow is falling heavier by the minute and there is hardly a cab to be had."

"All the better to suit my purpose, my friend," he replied, patting me on the shoulder. "By the way, I would be most obliged if you would remain free this evening after dinner. Formal dress, if you please."

Before I could question our destination he whipped a black scarf, about his face, muffling it against the cold, grabbed up a four foot shillelagh with a heavy knob from the stand by the door and departed into the dreary London afternoon.

Chapter Eleven

I spent the next few hours organizing my notes of the Clemens' affair, then settled into my chair by the fire with the latest copy of *The Strand* magazine. One of my favourite authors, F. Anstey, had a story in this issue called *The Brass Bottle*. Anstey was a neighbour of mine while Mary and I lived in Kensington. His actual name is Thomas Anstey Guthrie, and he is a well-known comic novelist. His story *Vice Versa* (1882) with its topsy-turvy substitution of a father for his schoolboy son, at once made his reputation as a humorist of an original type. As I began my own writing career, I took many lessons from reading the likes of Anstey, Dumas, and Dickens.

At five-thirty, I found that I had dozed off and was being shaken gently by our landlady who had come 'round to enquire about dinner. I answered in the affirmative, informing her that I would be going out afterwards, so the sooner, the better.

Once filled with the good Mrs. Hudson's repast, I brushed off, changed into my formal wear and waited for my friend. At seven-fifteen a knock on my door revealed a man bundled up in his livery and stating that he had orders to pick me up. He also handed me a note which I quickly read. It was from Holmes who stated thusly:

Watson,

I've arranged a pleasant evening for you to view 'Mark Twain' tonight. The young man accompanying you is an observant fellow and I wish you both to keep an eye on Clay and any other activity that arouses your suspicions. I will endeavour to meet you

there but if I am delayed I shall rejoin you at Baker Street
afterward. The rest of your company is window-dressing to keep
Clay from being suspicious, should he observe you.

Holmes

I slipped on my top hat and overcoat, took up my umbrella
and followed the driver to the waiting coach. Descending the
steps of our lodgings, I was naturally curious as to who my
companions would be. The Baker Street irregulars seemed
unlikely at such a formal gathering, although I've no doubt
they would enjoy any stories Clemens told about Tom Sawyer
or Huckleberry Finn.

When the coachman opened the door for me I was
pleasantly surprised to find myself greeted by none other
than Adelaide Savage, George and Marina.

I immediately doffed my hat and said, "Adelaide!
Children! What a pleasant surprise!"

As I settled in to a seat next to George, across from his
mother and sister, Adelaide returned my greeting. "John, it is
so good to see you, and how nice of Mr. Holmes to arrange
this entertainment for us."

"I confess I am flabbergasted to see you. Holmes told me
nothing of his scheme except for the note I just received. What
did he communicate to you?"

She flashed that winning smile that I remembered so well.
"His request came to us by messenger as well. Apparently he
requires George to assist you in the observation of some
person of interest in the Clemens' burglary? He did assure me
that there would be no danger, for it was to be observation
only. After all the two of you have done for us, I could hardly
refuse so generous an offer. We had no hope of obtaining
tickets for 'Mark Twain', but these arrived with his message."

She pulled four tickets from her bag and handed them to
me. They were excellent box seats. From what I remembered
of the Theatre Royal, they would be in the closest box to stage
left.

"These are wonderful seats!" I proclaimed. "Of course, Holmes does maintain his theatrical connections, so I shouldn't be surprised."

"Well, whatever the reason, I am grateful and looking forward to an exciting evening," she replied.

At this point George spoke up, "What are we looking for, Dr. Watson?"

Not wishing to alarm his mother, I gave a rather vague explanation, "There is a gentleman, by the name of John Clay, who claims to be a duke, but has a rather shady past as a convicted thief. He is staying in the room below Mr. Clemens. He says he was in for most of the evening on the night of the burglary, but he has no witnesses to this alibi. Holmes is convinced that the fire escape was central to the theft and thus it is possible that Clay could have gained access by this method with no one the wiser."

"What does this have to do with our going to the theatre tonight?" queried his mother.

Remembering our afternoon conundrum, I responded, "Holmes is still trying to ascertain the motive for the theft. If it was Clay, then his attendance at tonight's performance may give us a clue as to why he wanted those papers. We should be looking for anyone he talks to, whether he takes notes, or any other suspicious activity."

"Are we sure he will be there tonight? How will we find him?" asked George.

"When we interviewed him he mentioned that he was attending this performance of Mr. Clemens," I answered. "I have my opera glasses and, if he is still portraying himself as the Duke of Dartford, he is very likely to be seated in one of the high priced boxes. Hopefully he will be in our line of sight."

We soon pulled up to the four green and red brick double columns that held the Royal's portico, protecting patrons from the weather as they entered. Fortunately the snowfall had ceased with the setting of the sun. We were able to descend from our coach and enter the theatre with a minimum of fuss.

The Theatre Royal in Drury Lane is in its fourth incarnation, the present structure having been built in 1812. The original theatre came about after the eleven year long Puritan Interregnum, which had seen the banning of pastimes regarded as frivolous, such as theatre. With the return of the monarchy in the person of Charles II in 1660, Letters Patent were issued to two parties licensing the formation of new acting companies. One of these went to Thomas Killigrew, whose company became known as the King's Company, which built a new theatre in Drury Lane. The new playhouse opened in 1663 and was known, from the beginning, as the Theatre Royal.

We crossed the marble floor of the foyer with its black and white tiles and opulent crystal chandeliers, checked our hats, coats and umbrellas and proceeded to our seats. The ushers, upon seeing our tickets, treated us like royalty. We soon found ourselves escorted into the special box so near to the stage.

We met another pleasant surprise upon our arrival. Already seated in two of the front row chairs were Clemens' wife, Olivia and his daughter, Jean.

We exchanged greetings, I introducing Adelaide and her children as old friends. We sat Marina next to Jean and George next to his sister on the end opposite Mrs. Clemens. Adelaide and I sat behind Marina and George which made it convenient for Olivia Clemens to merely turn over her left shoulder to speak with us.

We had about ten minutes until the show was to begin. The author's wife kept up a running conversation with us while Jean drew Marina and George into a separate discussion.

"How is Mr. Holmes progressing with his investigation?" Mrs. Clemens asked.

My answer was far from satisfactory in my own mind, but then we had only been on the case for two days. "We have identified a few suspects," I replied, "but there is still the question of motive. Holmes spent this afternoon seeking out further information and may meet us here later, depending on where that information leads."

"Well, all I can say," replied our hostess, "is that in all our travels this is the most disturbing event we've run across. I mean, we've had luggage misplaced and there have been occasional items go missing, but to have someone deliberately break into our room to steal my husband's writings is beyond anything I could have imagined."

"If the case can be solved, Holmes is your man," I countered.

"Well, if nothing else, the opportunity to meet you and Mr. Holmes is a thrill my husband would have paid for. At least some good will have come out of it, even if the case isn't solved." She turned then and settled in as the last call for seating was made.

While the lights were still up, I retrieved my opera glasses from my pocket and began scanning the boxes where I thought Clay might be seated.

The interior of the Theatre Royal is far more opulent than its simple street facade would indicate. Gold fixtures, fine woods and maroon carpeting and tapestries, bespeak an elegance of appreciation for the fine arts.

It didn't take long to spot our quarry. Clay was seated almost directly across from us. As I sat in the farthest seat from the stage in our box, he was ensconced in the first seat of the second box from stage right on the same level. I leaned forward and handed the glasses to Adelaide's son.

"George" I spoke in low tones into his left ear, attempting to keep my voice from carrying to his sister on his right. "The gentleman in the second box across the way, the one with the red sash running diagonally across his chest, is the man we're looking for. You take the glasses and keep an eye on him occasionally. However, be sure to look all around the theatre, so that you appear to be just a curious young man taking in the view and not particularly spying on him."

"Yes, Doctor," answered my crony for the evening, "but wouldn't it be better if you watched him? I don't know what to look for."

"No, if he should spot me I don't want him thinking I'm here to spy on him. My being in the company of all of you should dissuade him from that assumption so long as I'm not the one looking at him with the opera glasses. Just notice if he speaks to anyone at length, or hands off a note to someone. I'll keep a casual eye on him as well. Fortunately, most of Mr. Clemens' performance is based upon what he says, rather than what he does, so we will still be able to appreciate the show without necessarily seeing all of it."

"Very well, Doctor," replied the college-bound lad as he took the glasses and began a casual circumvision of the audience.

I leaned back in my seat just as the house lights dimmed and found my arm encircled by the lovely wrist of my companion.

"I do hope you will enjoy the show, in spite of all this detective work you must be about," Adelaide whispered.

I looked down, patted her hand, then looked into her coquettish hazel eyes with my most charming smile and replied, "In your company it will be impossible not to."

Chapter Twelve

The stage was simply set, with a plain maroon curtain for a backdrop and no scenery. There was merely a lectern for 'Mark Twain' to stand behind and a table to one side and slightly forward, so that it would not be blocked from anyone's view by the lectern. The table held a water pitcher and glass as well as an ashtray. There was also a chair behind it. I supposed that this was for the author's benefit, as he was nearly 65 years old and should not be expected to stand for an extended period.

Clemens entered from stage right and walked slowly to the rostrum to a welcoming round of applause. He pulled some sheets of paper from his inner breast pocket and laid them on the table. He then strode behind the speaker's stand and waited for the laudation to subside.

When quiet once again reigned over the house, he began to speak.

While the following is the gist of the style of Clemens' talk, it is by no means complete. Even from memory and newspaper accounts, so much of his talk was extemporaneous and off-script I cannot guarantee its accuracy:

"Thank you for that fine welcome. As you can see I didn't have no one introduce me, preferring to do the honours myself, as I am the only one capable of performing the matter correctly. I was introduced to an audience once by a lawyer. This feller strode up to the podium, put his hands in his pockets and said." Ladies and gentlemen tonight we have with us Mr. Mark Twain, a humorist, who is remarkably funny".

"Now I took that as a compliment, as being remarkable for being a funny humorist. It would certainly lessen the popular opinion of me, were I to be an un-funny, humorist. However, what I found to be truly unusual, was that on that night, on that very stage, was the most remarkable sight anyone has seen in many a year ... a lawyer, with his hands in his *own* pockets.

"Actually I prefer to compliment myself. I do it all the time as a matter of course. I was born modest, but then I outgrew it.

"Therefore, I am here to tell you, that the two greatest living literary geniuses are Kipling and myself and I am proud to be in his company. He knows all there is to know about everything ... and I know all the rest.

"I am most grateful for your attendance on this evening after such a foul weather day. Usually when I am in London I am reminded so much of San Francisco. That is, until the fog burns off and I can see the city architecture and people driving on the wrong side of the road.

"That reminds me of a feller I worked with at the Chronicle in San Francisco. What was his name ...? Jackson, I believe. Yes, Carlton Jackson, of the Mississippi Jacksons, one of the finest families of the Mississippi delta. Well, Jackson was a delivery man for the Chronicle and he liked to play fast and loose with traffic laws when it came to which side of the street he would park his wagon on, 'cause if his customer was on the left he'd just naturally pull over there and make his delivery and anyone else on the road could just go around. Now, unlike your fair city, San Francisco is built on a bunch of hills and in the early mornin' anyone on the road would be drivin' up and down them hills, in and out of fog banks and strainin' to see. If they came upon that Chronicle delivery wagon sudden-like, they would likely veer to their left, assuming that it was on the right side of the road where it belonged. One time a carriage, drivin' lickety-split, came upon that wagon there in the fog and the driver yanked his horse's reins to the left just as Jackson was comin' out of the establishment that he had delivered his papers to and ... wait, it wasn't Jackson. No, no Jackson was a political cartoonist. Oh, it was Eldridge, that's it. Willie Eldridge. "He was one of the Virginia Eldridges. One of the oldest families in Richmond County. Could trace his ancestry clear back to the Jamestown colony.

"Now that reminds me, I have to thank you all for the fact that you folks couldn't just sit still on this here island of yours. Why, just a few years ago I took about to travelling around the world and writin' up stories for the newspapers back home, and thanks to your ancestor's colonizin' I had nary a day when I wasn't in some land or t'other that had inhabitants that spoke English, or something that resembled it close enough to be understood.

"I believe it was your own Oscar Wilde who said, 'We have really everything in common with America nowadays, except, of course, language.'" [1]

That drew a grand roar of laughter from the crowd and I stole a glance at Clay, who seemed to be thoroughly enjoying the show. Clemens paused, lit up a cigar and continued

"Now these days I can go from San Francisco to the Sandwich Islands and then on to Australia and hardly miss a word. Though there are some words in Australian that I never hear in any other English speaking country.

"From there I could sail to Malaysia, and on up to Hong Kong, then 'round to Burma, India and up the Red Sea and through the Suez Canal. Oh, wait a minute. Red Sea, Red ... it wasn't Eldridge now that I think on it. It was Packerman, 'Red'. That is, Charles 'Red' Packerman of the Texas Packermans, one of the finest families in the Lone Star state. One of his ancestors, his grandpappy I believe, fought with Sam Houston against General Santa Ana at San Jacinto. They say he caught

---

[1] *The Canterville Ghost* 1887

the general personally, disguised as private and hidin' in a swamp. Certainly not anything any British or American general would do. But then, Santa Ana didn't have the advantage of the English language in any form at all, so maybe this lack of education could excuse his performance.

"Of course my own military experience only consisted of two weeks drilling with the Missoura Volunteers of the Confederate Army, after which I decided that I wasn't cut out to be a soldier and took my leave of them fellers to join my brother and work for the Yankee government in the Nevada Territory, Of course, after my departure from the Confederate ranks, the Yankees won the war."

Clemens' performance went on in this vein for two and half hours with a twenty minute intermission. The audience seemed quite taken by his stories and manner. He frequently had to pause for the laughter to die down, a situation he often used to light a fresh cigar.

After the show, Mrs. Clemens invited us to accompany her backstage to join her husband. I noted Clay's departure. He appeared to be leaving by himself. I debated as to whether I should follow him or stand by my manners of courtesy and obligations as a gentleman and continue to escort Adelaide and her children. I retrieved Holmes' missive from my pocket and decided that he was expecting me back at Baker Street after the show if he had not made it to the theatre, thus I deduced that my obligations regarding Clay had ceased when the show ended.

However, I felt that I should at least keep an eye on Clay until he actually left the theatre. I told the ladies I would meet them backstage and took George with me as we made our way to the lobby. I stationed George near a restroom door where he could keep an eye on the cloakroom where, I assumed, Clay would retrieve his travelling attire. I waited outside, smoked a cigar and kept watch to note Clay's exit.

Due to the size of the crowd this took some little time and I had nearly finished my cigar when I caught the dubious duke's departure. He exited the theatre in the company of another gentleman. He was tall and thin with red hair and clean shaven. Together they hailed a cab and left in animated conversation.

I returned to the lobby and found George by the door where he had stopped, after following Clay to that point.

"Did you see him, Doctor?" asked the young lad.

"Yes, George," I answered, "though I did not recognize the gentleman with him. Did you see them meet?"

"Yes, sir, it appeared to be quite accidental. The duke had just retrieved his hat and cloak and when he turned he bumped into the other fellow. He seemed to recognize him and called him 'Scully'. Then he invited him to join him for a drink and waited until Scully claimed his own garments so they could leave together."

"Good show, George!" I exclaimed, "You've done well and I think that's enough for us to do for Mr. Holmes tonight. Let's go find the ladies. I'm sure you're anxious to meet Mark Twain."

We turned to walk together and then he paused a moment and asked me, quite sincerely in his youthful shyness, "Actually, Doctor, I was wondering if you could formally introduce me to his daughter?"

Ah, youth!

Chapter Thirteen

We were allowed backstage by the ushers as soon as I gave my name. Upon reaching Clemens' dressing room we were greeted warmly by the author who shook our hands vigorously.

"A pleasure to see you again, Dr. Watson," he stated animatedly. "I am sorry Mr. Holmes could not join us this evening."

"Trust me when I say, Mr. Clemens," I replied, "Holmes is actively pursuing clues in your case. I've no doubt he would have been here if some activity in that regard had not kept him away."

A barely perceptible throat clearing sound emanated from my young accomplice. I took the hint immediately. So as not to be too obvious and embarrassing to him, I summoned up my most formal manners.

"Mr. Clemens, allow me to present Mrs. Savage's son, George. George this is our host, the famous American author, Samuel Clemens."

George bowed and found himself responding to the handshake offered by 'Mark Twain' with a strong grip but a stuttering, 'a pleasure, sir'.

"The pleasure is mine, young feller. Sherlock Holmes spoke mighty highly of you when he dropped by to explain how he would be invading my box with visitors for tonight's show. I understand you have been enlisted in the task of trying to recover my stolen papers?"

"Yes, sir," George answered. "Although how much assistance I can offer I am sure I don't know."

"He's being far too modest," I interjected. "Already his observations have assisted both Holmes and myself in our tasks to find your thief."

"Well, thank you, George. I am most grateful for your help," replied the elderly author.

"And this," I continued, "is his wife, Olivia Clemens ..."
To whom George bowed, most properly.

"... and his daughter, Miss Jean Clemens."

At this, fortunately for the young man's purposes, Miss Clemens held out her gloved hand and George managed to take it gracefully and steady his voice as he looked into her bright blue eyes.

He responded, "A great pleasure, Miss Clemens."

Their eyes locked for a precious few seconds, until there was not a person in the room who did not realize what was happening.

Clemens broke the silence of the moment just before it became too awkward.

"Well, there's no use sitting around this draughty old dressing room all night," he stated, as he motioned us out of the room and toward the exit. "Reminds me of a theatre I played in Chicago. Now *that* was cold, I tell you. The act before me was a feller who had a dancing bear. Now during rehearsal that afternoon that was the blackest bear you ever did see, black as a crow in a coal mine.

"But that evening the temperature began to drop. The snow commenced to blowin' around, nigh unto a blizzard and the mercury fell faster than a stone down a dry well. By the time that there bear was set to perform, it was so cold that he danced out on the stage as white as a sheet and you'd a' swore he was a polar bear!"

We all laughed and soon found ourselves out in front of the theatre. Since our party had now swollen to seven, we decided to split up into two cabs and rejoin at the dining room of the Langham for a nightcap.

Clemens carefully manoeuvred the party so that all the young people went with him and his wife, which left Adelaide and me to share a private ride back to the hotel. Whether he did this for George's sake or mine I did not know and frankly, did not care.

It was a cold, dark and foggy night that surrounded the ride from the Theatre Royal to the Langham Hotel. Under such conditions the drive took us roughly twenty minutes.

Even though dressed accordingly against the frigid temperatures, Adelaide demonstrated no objection to my arm around her shoulders and, in fact, leaned her face into my shoulder as much as her chapeau would allow. Over the last couple of days it was as though an unspoken agreement had transpired between us. Feelings we had never voiced simply made themselves known by our actions.

When the cab stopped and the driver announced our arrival in front of the hotel, my companion looked up into my eyes. Without hesitation we kissed.[1]

At a clearing of the cabman's throat we separated, smiled knowingly and departed. I left the driver a nice tip with his fare and we walked arm in arm through the hotel lobby and on to the dining room.

We immediately spotted Clemens and company, and joined them at table. Everyone was all smiles, except for an odd look from Marina. Adelaide sat to the left of her daughter and I found myself between Adelaide and Olivia Clemens, who was next to her husband. The star of the evening's performance had somehow manoeuvred George between himself and Jean who was on Marina's right, which seemed to make everyone quite content.

Upon our arrival, a waiter appeared and took our orders for a variety of cakes, pies, teas and coffee. Clemens insisted on treating us all.

"The last time I was in London I was on a speaking tour with the object of retiring my debts, which had grown considerable due to some unfortunate investments. My circumstances are now quite comfortable and will be even more so if I can get your Parliament to meet with me and consider my proposed changes to the copyright law limitations which threaten the early works of authors

---

[1] Editor's note - I am sure that Watson, as a proper British gentleman, would never have included this action in his narration. Although it is in his notes, I believe he only jotted it down as a reminder of their first kiss. However, since it has been over a century, and my subsequent research reveals an on-going relationship between the good Doctor and Mrs. Savage, I felt it significant to the storyline to include.

everywhere. So, allow me to spend some of my profits from the kind audiences your islands have provided."[2]

I decided to forgo any argument, although it usually goes against my manners to allow a visiting guest to pay, especially since I felt responsible for the majority of the party.

We enjoyed our refreshments and laughed over the author's perceptions of the evening until we decided to call it a night, shortly after midnight.

As we exited into the lobby and made for the lift, who should come through the entrance but John Clay, himself.

The duke pretender, joined our party as we waited and I decided it was the better part of valor to make introductions.

After I had presented him to the American author, reluctantly, as the 'Duke of Dartford, John Clay', he responded in his most formal tone.

"Mr. Clemens, I particularly enjoyed your performance tonight. Your tour around the English speaking world was most delightful."

"Well, thank you, Duke," replied Clemens, "I appreciate it when the upper classes take enjoyment at my common attempts at humour."

The arrival of the lift interrupted this conversation. Since we were a large party, Clemens waved me and the Savages on and stayed behind with his family, continuing to speak with Clay.

We arrived at the fourth floor quickly and I escorted Adelaide and her children to their suite. The children proceeded ahead of us, George taking the key from his mother and opening the door. He and Marina went on in as Adelaide and I stopped at the entrance.

"Thank you for a lovely evening, John. Would you care to come in for a nightcap?" she asked.

I was about to answer in the affirmative, for I didn't want this evening to end, when Marina's voice sang out from within, "Are you coming, Mother?"

---

[2] Clemens would get his meeting with Parliament in June 1900 and argue for an extension of copyrights from 42 years to 'perpetuity'.

The tone in the young lady's voice was full of impatience and dampened the mood immediately. I decided that a strategic retreat was called for.

"I would love nothing better, Adelaide," I replied, wistfully, "but we seem to be keeping your children from their beds."

"They're certainly not children anymore," she replied petulantly, "They don't need their mummy to tuck them in and Marina seems to have misplaced her manners."

"I would imagine the sudden realization of seeing you, arm in arm with a man other than her father, has caught her off guard. I admit it has caught me somewhat off guard myself."

A smile spread across her face, "I confess to being rather surprised as well, John. But, I also confess to being excited at the possibilities before us."

"Mother?" Came another cry from within.

"You'd better go before she wakes the whole floor," I said. "I should get back to Baker Street to see what Holmes has been up to. I'll see you again soon, I promise."

I leaned forward and kissed her cheek, which she returned in kind.

"I'll hold you to that, Doctor," she smiled and stepped across her threshold, gently closing the door.

Just then the lift doors opened and the Clemens family disembarked. As we passed each other, Clemens gave his wife the key and sent her on ahead to their suite while he lingered to speak with me.

"I trust your evening went well, Dr. Watson?"

"Very well, Mr. Clemens," I replied. "Actually much better than I had expected."

"Please, call me Sam," he answered. "I know it doesn't seem to be the British way, but in my country we generally call our friends by our first names. Having read your works and now meeting you, I feel like we're old friends."

I smiled and replied, "Then I shall bow to your wishes, Sam, and you must feel free to call me John."

"Now I hadn't thought of that," he responded, with a quizzical look on his face. "Seeing your name in print so often it seems odd not to call you Watson or Doctor." Then he brightened, "How would you feel about 'Doc', Doctor?"

I replied with a small laugh, "If that pleases you, Sam, be my guest."

"Wonderful!" he exclaimed. "So, Doc, did you learn anything tonight that might help Holmes find my papers?"

"Well," I replied, "I did notice Mr. Clay meeting with a gentleman I do not know. I intend to report that to Holmes and see what he can make of it."

"You mean that there duke feller is a suspect?" the author responded, with no little astonishment.

I obviously had not realized that Holmes had not imparted this information to my American literary colleague. I decided to refrain from revealing Clay's past and chose a more tactful way out.

"He occupies the suite directly below yours, Mist...uh, Sam. That would certainly give him access to the same fire escape that the burglar used."

"He just don't seem the type to go climbin' up and down fire escapes. Besides, what would a duke want with my scribblin's?"

"Motive has been the big question from the beginning," I replied. "I believe if Holmes can puzzle that out, we'll find ourselves much closer to catching your thief."

"Well, good luck, Doc. I'd best be getting' off to bed myself. Give Mr. Holmes my best."

He shook my hand and departed toward his rooms. I called for the lift to return to the lobby and exited the hotel. I was soon in a hansom winding my way back through a light snowfall to Baker Street. Upon arrival, I found my friend in his mouse-coloured dressing gown, threadbare and in need of replacement after all these years, stretched out in front of a crackling fire, smoking his pipe and deep in thought.

Chapter Fourteen

I discarded my outer garments and settled into my chair across from my detective friend. Retrieving a pipe of my own, I filled it with my favourite Arcadia tobacco and waited for him to speak.

He did not look at me for some moments. In fact, I thought that perhaps his trance-like thought process had failed to register my arrival. Then, without seeming to look at me, he finally spoke softly.

"Watson, my dear friend, your evening was far more stimulating than I had imagined. Yet, I perceive that you still accomplished your mission in spite of such happy distractions."

Refusing to be flustered by his remark, I simply replied, "It was all by your arrangement, Holmes. After all these years of our acquaintance my actions should have been predictable to such a seasoned deductive reasoner as yourself."

He finally looked straight at me and smiled. "**Your** actions, yes my trusted friend. However, I confess I did underestimate the depth of feelings of the fair Mrs. Savage."

"And how do you know the depths of her feelings?" I replied defensively, "Were you hidden in some corner of the theatre or the hotel dining room. Oh, wait, perhaps you were the cabbie who drove us? Really Holmes you can be quite intolerable."

He gave a small chortle, "Not at all, my good Doctor. In fact the majority of my afternoon and evening has been spent rather far from the venues you enjoyed."

"I know I am going to be sorry I asked, but then how did you ..."

Holmes waved me to silence and answered my unfinished question.

"The fair lady's makeup has smudged the right shoulder of your overcoat," he stated, pointing to the coat rack by the door where I had hung it up. "So much so that it could only have occurred during the cab ride, in which you were obviously alone, without the company of her children. They must have taken a different conveyance with the Clemens family. The sleeve of your right arm is unnaturally creased where she held on to you for some time, likely during the theatre performance, and there is a trace of lipstick on your cheek and even a small bit in your moustache."

With colour rising in my cheeks I attempted to change the subject.

"Then how could you possibly believe I accomplished my task with such distractions going on?"

"Really, Watson, I am not blind. As you sat down just now you removed your notebook from your breast pocket and laid it on the table. I could see you have marked the page of tonight's reporting with your pencil."

He leaned forward, setting his pipe aside for the moment.

"So, Doctor, have you convicted John Clay, or exonerated him?"

I retrieved my notebook and told Holmes the methods by which young George and I kept a clandestine eye on the so-called duke.

"Well done," he interjected.

"Thank you, Holmes," I responded with a little pride, then continued.

"Now Clay was alone during the performance, although I confess we could not get 'round to the other side of the theatre to catch where he had gone during intermission. However we did spot him leaving a men's room before returning to his seat. Unless he had meeting in the loo I doubt anything untoward occurred."

I then told him how George had witnessed the apparent accidental meeting of Clay and Scully and how I had seen them leave in the same cab.

"Scully was tall and thin ..."

"… with red hair, clean shaven and roughly forty years old?" Holmes finished.

"Yes," I replied, closing my notebook, "Do you know him?

"We have not been formally introduced but I have seen him speak before Parliament. He possesses an excellent voice and a penchant for story-telling. He is the Viscount Scully of Elysian Park and is a strong advocate for greater government involvement in caring for widows and orphans.

"Then his connection to Clay may merely be in regards to the Cornwall Orphanage." I observed.

"Most likely," replied Holmes, who smiled, rather devilishly I thought. "But I trust that the rest of your evening's activities will far outweigh any disappointment regarding Clay."

Refusing to be drawn in to such a discussion I instead asked, "And what of your day, Holmes. Have you made any progress toward catching our thief?"

Instead of answering immediately, he walked to the sideboard and poured a brandy for each of us. He handed one to me and sat down, settled back in his chair, crossed his long legs and re-lit his pipe. As the blue/grey haze filled the air above his head, he began a narration of his day's activities.

"My first stop, Watson, was Scotland Yard. I met with our friend, Inspector Hopkins to ascertain any progress he may have made on Clemens' behalf.

"He confirmed Ward James' dinner with Sir Edwin on the night in question. Now his investigations have closed in on the rest of the occupants who were on Clemens' floor during the evening of the theft, but have since left the hotel. He should complete that task soon. However, he is currently attempting to track the whereabouts of the gentleman who was in the suite above Clemens, a fellow who registered under the name of A. W. Smith. Some member of the hotel staff told Hopkins he believed the man was an actor."

I chimed in, "An actor might have use for Clemens' papers, if he wished to create an act similar to the 'Mark Twain' performance that I witnessed tonight."

"A distinct possibility, Watson. Of course to perform such an act he would have to remove himself far from Clemens' presence in order to avoid confrontation regarding the source of his materials. While our American friend is in England this actor would need to take himself off to the Continent at least."

"Yes, Holmes, but in America he could roam rather freely over a large portion of the country and maintain himself hundreds, or even thousands of miles distant from Clemens. I've read that the Vaudeville circuit is rather extensive there and imitators of famous persons are quite popular."

"You echo Hopkins' thoughts precisely, Doctor. He has put the word out to all ports with American bound ships to be on the lookout for this fellow. He has officers checking the passenger manifests for any such person sailing for the Continent as well.

"I, on the other hand, took this information to Irving[1] after I left the Yard. He will use his vast theatrical connections to try and ascertain the fellow's whereabouts."

Nodding in understanding I enquired, "I suppose that was how you came about obtaining our theatre tickets for this evening."

"You were using tickets reserved for Sir Henry, Watson," he replied. "They are normally the artists' guest box but Clemens was using only two of them. Irving's invited party was delayed by blizzards to the north so I was able to obtain his seats for you. I felt that it would serve our purposes to see just how much interest Clay took in Clemens' performance."

"That explains the two empty seats," I said. "But you had already asked me to assume formal attire for an evening out before you left Baker Street. How did you know you would obtain those tickets?

"I did not know, Watson. Had I not the good fortune of Irving's generosity I was going to ask Clemens for backstage passes for you and myself, so that we could wander the theatre freely and keep an eye out for anyone suspicious."

---

[1] Sir Henry Irving, proprietor of the Lyceum theatre and England's premier actor, producer and stage director of the era.

"I see," I replied. "I assume you were unable to join us due to trails leading elsewhere?"

"Ah, there we come to the bulk of my evening. Since Sanford's establishment has arisen in two of our suspects alibis, I deemed it prudent to take my investigation there. Fortunately, the cue stick skills I developed in my university days have not completely rusted away. I was able to give a fair account of myself against various opponents. It is indeed a popular establishment and this evening's participants were a most interesting group."

"Thurston and I play there on occasion," I recalled. "It can be rather boisterous but there is no shortage of tables, so we rarely have to wait for a game."

"You would not have found it so tonight, my friend," Holmes answered. "Apparently it has become the venue of choice for Olympic hopefuls, as there are several men hoping to demonstrate their skills at the Paris Exhibition this summer."

"I was not aware of that, Holmes. Was there anyone there whom I would know?"

"Your friend, Thurston was on hand, and so was the current champion, Charles Dawson.[2] More interestingly, young Mr. James and his friend, Reese were there, as were Gilliam and our gun-toting reporter, Hodges."

"Hodges?" I questioned. "What was he doing there?"

"Apparently he was there in his capacity as a reporter, seeking out stories for the Paris Exhibition and Olympic Games. He talked with several of the players and took copious notes. He even played against a few of them , noting their various strategies and techniques."

"That sounds legitimate," I countered. "Was there anything that happened that might help our case?"

"Gilliam played with several fellows who are not of stellar reputation. I discovered a couple of them to be rogues who entice players into wagering. After losing and seeming inept, they come on as desperate and beg for a larger bet at which

---

[2] British billiard champion 1899, 1900, 1901 and 1903.

point they expose their true skill and clean out their mark's purses."

I grinned sardonically, "Yes, the American term is 'pool shark'. Unfortunately, that is becoming a common practice at many billiard parlours, which is why Thurston and I prefer to play at his club where such scoundrels are quickly shown the door."

Holmes waved his pipe at me and nodded, "I bow to your expertise. While I did not hear anything incriminating, I could not be everywhere at once. James and Reese only played against each other and talked rather freely on a myriad of subjects. When they parted, James told Reese to give his regards to Sir Edwin."

I thought that over for a moment and asked, "Isn't Sir Edwin quite a bit older than these young men? It hardly seems they would travel in the same circles."

"He is more of an age with James' father, the Earl," Holmes agreed. "It may merely stem from a long term family friendship, but I do plan to explore that avenue a bit."

"So, nothing concrete for either of our night's endeavors." I responded, knocking out my pipe and reaching for my brandy.

"We sift through the dust of our clues, Watson. If the right pieces fall into place we make clay. Strengthen the clay with straws of facts and we have the bricks that build our case."

"You're waxing poetic, Holmes," I stated.

"Am I?" he replied reflexively, then, with a quick glance at my overcoat, continued, "It must be all the romance in the air."

Chapter Fifteen

The next morning I awoke late to find Holmes gone, which meant to me that he had found inspiration to seek out a new track in our case. On the table was a note telling me that if I had any patients to attend to he did not anticipate requiring my services until the afternoon. However, if any message arrived from either Irving or Hopkins I was to feel free to act upon it and leave him a note as to my plans.

I requested a hearty breakfast from Mrs. Hudson and devoured it and the morning edition of the Telegraph, simultaneously. Within its pages I found a typical review of Clemens' theatrical performance:

> Samuel Clemens, as Mark Twain, was thoroughly entertaining at the Theatre Royal last night. I haven't the slightest idea what he spoke about, but I left the theatre with ribs sore from laughter and the crowd in general seemed in agreement.

I agreed wholeheartedly. Clemens' meandering monologue weaved tales of comedy, suspense and downright absurdity as he took us along on his unique world travels. I cannot imagine he repeats this act word for word. It all seems to flow freely and goes wherever his imaginative mind takes it at any given point.

I did have one patient that I felt I should check on and so fortified myself against the cold and took up my medical bag. Just as I exited our abode out into the light snowfall, a growler stopped in front of me at the curb. Out stepped Frederick MacDonald, a long time acquaintance of ours with the Metropolitan Police Force.

"Mr. Mac," I called out above the muffler protecting my throat and chin, "What brings you out on this chilling day? I thought retirement would find you in front of a warm fire with a hot cup of tea."

"Aye, Dr. Watson," he answered in his thick brogue, "I found retirement a bothersome bore. I may not have the strength of my youth to chase about the criminal classes of the City, but I can still run errands and free up those who do."

"You bring a message, then?" I enquired.

"Aye, for Mr. Holmes or yourself, Doctor, from Inspector Hopkins," he replied as he handed me an envelope.

I tore it open and found a missive that was short on detail but brought significant news. It read:

> Have eliminated all hotel guests who left on Friday, except Smith. Re-checking hotel staff backgrounds. Please advise progress on your end.
>
> Hopkins

"Well, this is some good news at any rate. Thank you," I stated to the retired policeman.

"Any reply for the Inspector, Doctor?"

I thought a moment and finally said, "Tell him that Holmes is off investigating this morning. He is using his theatrical connections to try and find Smith. I am sure he will inform the Inspector of any progress."

MacDonald nodded and turned to re-board his cab, then called to me, "May I drop ye somewheres, Doctor?"

Realizing that my patient's home would require only a slight detour for his trip back to Scotland Yard, I accepted his invitation and climbed aboard next to him, sharing the travelling rug provided by the cabman.

We discussed his family as the cab ploughed through the newly fallen snow that had piled up to about three inches during the night. His son was doing well as a major in the Royal Marines. He proudly boasted of his grandson's acceptance into Harvard law school in Massachusetts.

"Never cared much for solicitors myself, but Jack has a great heart for helping the poor and he's always wanted to live in America. He's stayin' with my daughter, Kathleen and her husband, Tom, in Boston."

"I envy you your family, Mac," I said, a little wistfully. "It's a fine thing for a man to have descendants to be proud of."

"Aye, it is. A pity your poor Mary passed away so young," he stated sympathetically. Then, with that bluntness that only the elderly can get away with, he asked, "Ha'e ye not thought o' marryin' again, Doctor?"

The question caught me off guard and, before I realized what I was saying I had answered.

"Actually, Mac, recent events have brought that possibility into my thoughts."

"Well now, that would be a fine thing," he answered. "A pity Mr. Holmes chooses to remain a bachelor. I can only imagine what gifts his offspring might possess."

I barely heard this statement for I was lost in the fact that I had actually given voice to thoughts that were only fleeting up until now. The next thing I knew the cabman was pulling up at my patient's house and announcing our arrival.

I tossed him up a coin for his trouble and bade farewell to my semi-retired companion. Having left the confines of the travelling rug, the cold bit hard through my legs as I limped up the walk to the door. Fortunately, it was answered quickly by the housekeeper. She took my outer garments and offered to bring me some hot tea.

I accepted gratefully and was asked to wait in the parlour while she informed my patient, Mr. Alston, of my arrival.

Thoughts of Adelaide filled my mind as I reflected on the statement I had made in the cab and sipped my tea. Was I really contemplating such a life-changing step, or was I merely enjoying having some female companionship, so long missing from my life?

Alston's housekeeper announced that he was ready to receive me and I set my teacup down and proceeded up the stairs.

The gentleman was lying in bed, bundled up against the chill and a fire blazed hot on the hearth.

I performed my examinations for his flu-like symptoms and determined that they had just about run their course. I advised him and his housekeeper he should continue to guard against chill, apply warm compresses for his chest and drink lots of liquids, especially hot soups.

Assuring them that I would check on him again in a few days, I donned my hat and coat once again. I was fortunate to have a cab respond quickly to my whistle, as I stepped out into the snowfall.

The ride back to Baker Street was slower, with frequent pauses to wait for the special wagons that were attempting to clear the snow from the streets. This gave me more time to ponder my situation with Adelaide.

Assuming that I was, in fact, contemplating a matrimonial relationship, what was she thinking? Was this time together just the enjoyment of companionship for two people in the throes of middle age, without love for a long time? Was she suddenly realizing that, with George off to school and Marina of an age to marry, she would soon find herself alone and was fearful of that prospect?

My head was spinning with all the possibilities. By the time I had arrived at Baker Street I had determined that, as Holmes would say, speculation was useless without data. I resolved to broach the subject with Adelaide when next we met.

*****

I had been absent less than two hours so there was no lunch yet to occupy my time. I accepted some hot coffee from Mrs. Hudson, stoked the fire and contemplated Holmes' reference books that filled the shelves of our sitting room. Hoping to feel useful, I pulled one down that contained the 'S's' and began perusing it for A.W. Smith.

The first name my eyes were drawn to, of course, was 'Culverton Smith', the uncle and murderer of Adelaide's husband. This naturally set my memories wandering to my

106

initial introduction to the lady whose company now stirred my heart.

It may have been my newly married status at the time, but, like my sweet wife Mary, I recalled seeing Mrs. Savage as a 'lady in distress'. In her case, much more so, for she was being evicted from her home with two young children to care for.

Mary had treated me like a knight in shining armour at the conclusion of her case. Though Holmes had done the deductive work, we had equally shared the danger. A harrowing race down the Thames after Jonathan Small and his most dangerous companion, the little Andaman Islander, Tonga. His poison dart passed between Holmes and myself, then struck the bridge of our police launch at the same time our pistols rang out and brought him down.

The mutual attraction Mary and I felt for each other had manifested itself early in the case, but this brush with death brought our feelings to the fore and we immediately became engaged.

In the Savage case, I was still feeling that sense of 'knight to the rescue' in the work Holmes and I performed, but not the stirring emotions of love that had helped motivate me to gain justice for Mary. I would have described Mrs. Savage as attractive, had I thought of it at the time, but I was a happily married man with no other thought than to obtain justice for this widow and her children.

Physically, Adelaide and my wife shared their blonde hair, hazel eyes and above average height in common. Whereas Mary was a willowy five foot, six inches with a quiet manner, Adelaide, while not so slight and delicate, is about an inch taller and possesses a more outgoing personality.

I wondered at this resemblance. Was I seeing Adelaide as what Mary would have been like, had she lived these past ten years? And what of Adelaide's vision of me? Victor and I shared the same height and build. Our largest difference would be his dark curly hair versus my light brown and now greying, wavy hair. He was clean-shaven while I have had my moustache since my military days.

I did not know him prior to his death, only that he had succumbed to a weakness for drugs, that his uncle both encouraged and attempted to use to hide his murderous scheme.

Was Adelaide seeing me as the man she had hoped Victor would become?

Lost in this reverie of analysis, I had not been aware of Holmes' return until his voice suddenly descended over my shoulder.

"You are quite over-thinking the situation, Watson."

Startled, I flinched and nearly dropped the volume that was in my lap. Turning, I saw Holmes backing away from me and retrieving one of his pipes from the mantle.

"I have always left the fair sex to you, my friend," he stated matter-of-factly, "but if you care to hear it, I would advise you on your thoughts."

Setting the book on the table, I gazed up at the tall figure of Holmes as he lit his shag.

"Holmes, how could you possibly know my thoughts?" I queried.

"Really, old fellow," he droned, "Once I ascertained that you were perusing the 'S' section of my references it was simplicity itself to follow your train of thought.

"Obviously, you were hoping to find some notation on 'A.W. Smith', not knowing that I had already checked for it last night while you slept and found nothing. Coming to the 'Smiths' you could not help but notice Culverton Smith, who was the cause of Mrs. Savage's unhappiness that brought her into our sphere.

"The faraway look upon your face, as you fingered the pocket watch given to you as a wedding present by your beloved Mary, surely advertised your thoughts of her memory. The alternating smiles and frowns that passed over your countenance in succession, were indicative of a struggle in your own mind.

"The obvious physical resemblance between your wife and Mrs. Savage would certainly attract you to her. You are wondering if it is merely that resemblance that draws you, or if something deeper is afoot."

I lit one of my Bradley's and took a puff on the cigarette before answering. I was a bit shaken at the accuracy of his deductions, in spite of our long years of friendship and the multiple times he has demonstrated this power.

Attempting to make light of it I accused him, "Holmes, you've been reading Freud's articles in my medical journals."

He fell into a chair and exhaled his smoke loudly, "Bosh! Freud bends every situation to fit his theories and discounts other factors that would have obvious influence on behaviour. I am looking at your situation through deductive reasoning, my friend."

I acquiesced and leaned forward with my elbows on my knees, cigarette ash in danger of falling to Mrs. Hudson's carpet.

"And your advice, dear fellow?"

"Love at first sight is fine for the poets of this world, but in actuality it is the rarest of commodities. Your instance with the fair Miss Morstan was one of those unique situations which no one should expect to find twice in a lifetime, for once is rare in itself.

"I have never spoken of my emotions in your hearing, Watson and I will not do so now except to say that, after you married, I was occasionally envious of the happiness that you had found. That level of joy has always been foreign to me and I expect always will be.

"But as I see those emotions sparking to life within you again, I will venture to act as your logical conscience and merely state that you must not rush this relationship. Adelaide is not Mary. She will not act, nor react like her, as much as you may wish to see that.

"However, both of you are older and, hopefully, wiser and see the world differently than in your youth. You also know that time is the great equalizer. We've both seen cases where a rush to judgment, and resulting actions, have proven disastrous."

I sighed, "So you are saying we should move slowly and let the relationship develop over time to ensure its veracity."

He crossed one long leg over the other and folded his hands over his knee. "I am, first of all, apologizing, for it is none of my business. However, as an exercise in logical deduction it has occupied my thoughts recently and I have shared my hypothesis with you. Being the expert on women that you are, I am sure your own thoughts will be every bit as viable as mine, if not more so."

"Holmes, you are insufferable!" I cried.

"Indubitably," he answered, "but I have had a busy morning with no breakfast and would like to share some of Mrs. Hudson's hot beef stew with you for lunch, as we are expecting a visitor this afternoon."

"Who's coming by? Hopkins?" I asked.

"All in good time," he replied, as he strode to the doorway and called downstairs to let our landlady know we were ready for lunch.

"For now," he stated, as he came back and sat down, "let us compare our morning's adventures."

Chapter Sixteen

I handed him the message from Hopkins.

He read it quickly, nodded and replied, "It is as I expected. The other guests were not likely suspects from what I was able to glean. It will be interesting to track down this Smith fellow though."

"You think that his occupation as an actor may give him motive?" I asked.

"With no ransom demand, the motive for the theft of Clemens' papers narrows to its usage by an inscrutable actor, writer or publisher," he answered. "Either that, or a blackmailer is threatening someone other than Clemens."

"What if someone merely wanted to lay hold of them to destroy them?" I challenged.

"If destruction were their purpose they could have avoided the risk of getting caught in the act by merely throwing them into the fire that was burning brightly in Clemens' sitting room," he parried.

At that moment, Mrs. Hudson arrived with a tray filled with a steaming tureen of stew with bowls, bread and butter. We thus sat down to a hearty meal.

While we dished up our servings, I tossed out one more theory, based on a chance remark of Olivia Clemens the previous night.

"What if they weren't stolen at all?" I posed.

"What?" Holmes responded, distractedly.

"Olivia Clemens mentioned last night her husband would have paid for an opportunity to meet you. What if he staged this whole thing, as a chance to see you in action?"

Holmes seemed to mull that over as he sliced off a piece of bread and slathered it with butter. Finally he answered, "I would not put it past him, Watson. After all, he is prone to theatrics like myself. I believe he cannot resist the dramatic at times. However, from my talks with Hopkins, I believe that Clemens was genuinely surprised to learn that I was alive and well. In addition, I found no indication of his briefcase being taken anywhere else in the suite. Something was lowered to the alley and it banged into Clay's railing on the way down. That sound, I am sure, was mixed in with the thunder he spoke of.

"No, Watson, this took some planning beyond a mere lark on Clemens' part. Someone targeted those papers."

I nodded, then asked, "But who would even know he had them, Holmes?"

He smiled, "Our American friend is a very garrulous fellow, Doctor. I'm sure it came up in many of his conversations. He may even mention it during his stage performance, depending on his topic for the evening."

"Yes, I suppose you're right," I answered. "Then we're back to motive again."

"As always, old friend, but the gentleman I am expecting may be able to shed some light on that for us."

I was about to enquire again as to whom this benefactor might be when Mrs. Hudson knocked on the open door and began to announce him. Before she could utter a word however, the man himself gently set her aside and crossed our threshold.

He looked, for all the world, like Father Christmas, with long white hair and beard under a bowler, scarf and heavy tweed overcoat. However, his deep cockney-accented voice belied this impression and I recognized it at once.

"There now, Mrs. 'Udson," he stated, "the guvnor's expectin' me. Just toddle your pretty self off to that sweet-smellin' kitchen of yours. Say, you wouldn't have any more o' that delicious lookin' stew about would ye?"

Our forever patient landlady looked at Holmes who nodded and then she sighed and answered, "I'll bring another bowl."

As she left, our guest turned to Holmes again, "And I don't suppose a gent could get a drop o' brandy on a chilly afternoon such as this?"

Holmes, obligingly stood, stepped to the sideboard and poured a generous glass of the elixir, motioning the man to take his vacated seat for the repast that Mrs. Hudson would soon bring forth.

"So, Johnson," he said, as he set the glass down on the table, "I see you took precautions to avoid anyone associating you with us. I congratulate you on your excellent disguise."

With some effort Johnson divested himself of his overcoat and hung it with his hat and scarf on the stand by the door. He then proceeded to remove his wig and beard in one smooth motion and hung them up as well.

"It would do neither of us no good if anyone was to figure out that we was associates, Mr. 'Olmes. My life wouldn't be worth tuppence and ye would lose my very valuable services."

He paused at this remark and raised enquiring eyebrows at my friend. Holmes took the not so subtle hint and dropped a five pound note next to the brandy glass.

"Bless ye, sir" Johnson replied, folding the note neatly, kissing it and stuffing it into a pocket within his waistcoat as he sat down.

Shinwell Johnson[1] had become a reliable agent for Holmes, a remarkable feat in that he was once a dangerous villain, having served two terms at Parkhurst for his crimes. Now in his repentance, he used his vast knowledge of London's criminal underworld to keep abreast of activities that might interest the detective. There was not a nightclub, gambling house, opium den or other shady establishment where he was not welcome by his reputation, and such inroads often proved invaluable to my friend.

In appearance he was a large, coarse fellow, red-faced with a mean look. The only hint to his cunning mind was a pair of vivid black eyes which took in everything about him.

---

[1] Shinwell Johnson also appears in the canonical story, *The Illustrious Client,* published in1902

"And what does my *associate* have to tell me this afternoon?" Holmes asked.

"As ye requested, Mr. 'Olmes, I've 'ad me ear to the pavement, doors, walls and windows and there ain't nary a breath about them papers yer seekin'. I even let it out that I had a buyer if they was for sale and not a bite nowhere's. Not a soul's taken credit for the 'eist neither. And somethin' like that, a job at the Langham? That's beggin' to be bragged on by whoever did it. No, sir, this weren't pulled off by any local boys, I'd swear to it."

Just then, Mrs. Hudson arrived with another bowl and Johnson shovelled up a large helping of stew and began eating. Holmes had lit a cigarette and was pondering Johnson's report, then I asked a question.

"So, in your opinion, Johnson, this theft is the work of foreign agents or, at the very least, someone from outside of London's established underworld?"

"Must be, Doctor," he replied between mouthfuls of hot stew.

"What would you say to John Clay being involved?" I posed.

Holmes studied the man for his reaction, which was nonchalant at first.

"Clay's in Dartmoor prison," Johnson answered simply, as he spread butter lavishly upon a thick piece of bread.

"Clay was released on parole six weeks ago and is, in fact, staying at the Langham in the room directly below Clemens," I replied.

Johnson stopped his bread halfway to his mouth and looked at Holmes for confirmation. When Holmes nodded, he set the slice down and looked thoughtful.

"Well now, that'd be another story," the man pondered. "Without Moriarty or Moran, Clay would be on 'is own. I've 'eard 'e's got plenty of money waiting for 'im though. Don't know as there be a need for 'im to steal them papers. Unless he was lookin' for samples of Clemens' 'andwritin' so's 'e could forge some documents."

114

"It won't do," proclaimed Holmes. "For such a task he would only need a few papers which could have been removed and probably gone unnoticed for some time. There would be no need to steal the entire briefcase."

"Then I'd allow that Clay's not involved," replied Holmes' agent. "Stealin' fer ransom or blackmail ain't his bailiwick."

"All the same," added Holmes, "continue your enquiries regarding the theft of the papers and see what you can learn about a fellow named Gilliam. He's acting as Clay's valet, but they were in prison together."

"As you say, Mr. 'Olmes," Johnson responded, standing, stuffing his bread into his mouth then wiping his ample round face with a napkin. He finished off his brandy in one healthy gulp and donned his disguise and garments to venture once again out into the chilly afternoon.

With Johnson's departure, Holmes now deigned to fill me in on his morning activities.

"I spent a good deal of time looking into the law offices of Davis, Davis and Howard and young Mr. Reese," he recalled.

"Reese just joined the firm last year, having served his clerkship elsewhere. He did indeed, attend Cambridge with Ward James and they were quite close. Although James excelled on horseback at polo while Reese was a stellar wing on the rugby field, their personalities drew them together and they became fast friends. After school Reese, whose grades were outstanding, went on to study for law while the less cerebral James opted for a stint in her majesty's service until a bout with malaria forced him to muster out two years ago. He has since been assisting his father in the management of the estates at Roseboro. This has given him a healthy income and he travels to London quite frequently. He is unmarried, as is Reese, and they often make the rounds together enjoying the company of any number of ladies."

"So there seems to be no motive for either of them to steal Clemens' papers," I proffered.

"So it would seem," replied my friend. "However, James has been known to leave Roseboro, bound for some unknown destination on unspecified business. There is a rumour that he once returned from one of these trips with a bullet wound in his arm. I have been unable to corroborate that as yet."

"Intriguing," I responded, "but hardly conclusive to our case."

"Agreed," said the detective, "although this Reese is an interesting fellow. He does quite well as a barrister, but he does not come from a wealthy family. They are of moderate means and it was as much his athletic ability as his intellectual prowess that opened the door to Cambridge for him. Yet he currently lives in a desirable residence near Piccadilly that seems more conducive to a partner's income than his own."

"You suspect an illegitimate source of funds?" I queried.

"Perhaps not illegitimate," answered Holmes, "but at present unknown and therefore of interest until proven otherwise."

"So what is your next move, Holmes?"

"For now, I have shifted efforts towards this A.W. Smith fellow. Irving has his contacts searching it out and I expect to hear from him this afternoon, which is when I may require your assistance. I trust your patient is mending nicely?"

"The worst is over." Then I started, "How did you know I'd been to see a patient?"

"Come now, Watson," he replied "Not only were your outer garments still damp when I returned, but your medical bag as well. Since you were not gone long and were free of patient worries enough to concentrate on your relationship with Mrs. Savage, I concluded your patient is in no danger."

"Well and good, Holmes," I said, but then decided to throw a barb back at him. "By the way, Frederick MacDonald says you should have children."

Chapter Seventeen

"I beg your pardon?" he answered, quite astonished at the subject matter no doubt.

I repeated MacDonald's observation, to which Holmes merely grunted and stated, "I've no desire to be coping with adolescent offspring in my retirement years, Doctor. Thank you, no. The only caretaking I intend to engage in, at some future date, will be in regards to the study of bees on the Sussex Downs."

As far as he was concerned, that closed the matter and he changed the subject.

"Now, to more important matters. Though I still believe the thief came in through the front door and staged the rest, without proof I cannot discount the possibility that Smith may be involved. He could have used the fire escape, acting in concert with a partner in the alley. It may even be that he staged the scene to make it deliberately look staged so that we would discount the real sequence of events. "

"It all seems so diabolical, Holmes," I posed.

"The entire matter is ..."

A knock on the door and Mrs. Hudson's voice announcing the arrival of a telegram, interrupted his thought. He immediately leapt to her side and snatched the paper from her hand. I attempted to soothe her startled reaction at his abruptness with a 'thank you' and gently led her out the door.

Turning back to Holmes I admonished him for his rudeness, "Really, Holmes can you not even summon forth simple manners with poor Mrs. Hudson?"

"I'll apologize later, Watson. This is from Irving. His contacts have located our elusive Mr. Smith and we can find him performing at the Hippodrome Theatre in Bristol. Be a good fellow and check Bradshaw for the next train."

There was a departure for Bristol from Paddington Station at four-thirty that afternoon, which would make the 120 mile trip in five hours, due to the many stops along the way. An alternative would be to wait for an Express in the morning. It would reduce our travel to a mere three hours since it only stopped at Reading and Swindon on its way to Bristol.

When I relayed this information to Holmes he immediately cried out, "Then let us pack our overnight bags and be off, Watson. The sooner we track down this fellow the better, one way or the other."

"Naturally," I grumbled to myself, having much preferred to wait for the Express. I tried to dissuade him with the fact that, it being Monday, the theatre would be dark. There was no way for us to contact this fellow except at the theatre.

"Watson, you forget the knowledge I gained of the theatre in my youthful acting days. It is highly likely that we will find our quarry in rehearsal, if we arrive in time."

Surrendering to his will, I retreated to my room and began throwing some things together for a quick trip. As I did so I came to question one thing. I stepped to my doorway and called out to my companion.

"Holmes, shall I pack my revolver?"

Several ticks of the hall clock marked the time before he answered, "I trust it will not be needed, old fellow. But let us be prepared, just in case."

*****

We arrived at Paddington Station with ten minutes to spare. Fortunately the train was not particularly full at that hour, and when the locomotive made its opening lurch at the beginning of our journey we found that we had the compartment to ourselves.

Holmes lit his pipe as we picked up speed. A few straggling passengers still passed along the corridor. None attempted to join us, but suddenly my friend became most animated.

He stood and surreptitiously opened our door to take a peek along the corridor. Nodding to himself, he closed the door quietly and resumed his seat with a smile.

"What is that look, Holmes?" I asked, "Who did you see?"

"It appears our young friend, Mr. James, had a busy day, Watson. Instead of this morning's Express, he has been forced to make his return home with us on this rather slow mode of travel."

"What of it, Holmes?" I responded, "He told us he would be returning home today."

"Just a curiosity, Watson," he said. "If he knew he would be forced to take this train, why not wait until tomorrow's Express, which would be much more comfortable and still allow him to be back at Roseboro before lunchtime?"

"You could simply ask him, Holmes," I stated, as I unfolded my afternoon paper and began to read.

"I shall take that under consideration, Doctor," he replied. "However, we have a journey of several hours, so there is no need for immediate action."

He stretched his long legs out on his seat and leaned back into a corner to finish his pipe. Once he put it away he pulled his homburg down and closed his eyes. Whether in concentration or to take a short nap I was unable to ascertain until, after an hour's time, I decided to stretch my legs. I put down my paper. I softly mentioned that I was stepping out and he acknowledged my comment with a short wave of his hand.

While I strolled the corridor of the moving train, I noted various types of people in those compartments that were occupied. Primarily they seemed to be either well-dressed businessmen or families traveling to, or returning from, holiday.

I stealthily looked for young James and was rewarded for my efforts when I spotted him standing in a compartment at the far end of the car. What I did not expect, was the passenger who shared that compartment with him.

Through the window in the compartment door I was startled to see the figure of Miss Jean Clemens, standing and facing the young man. She was wagging a finger at him and had an extraordinary, agitated look upon her face as she shouted words I could not understand through the door. I watched, momentarily frozen by surprise. Then she suddenly slapped him with great enough force to stagger him to one side. He retained his feet though, and reached back to take her by both arms and force her down into her seat. At this point, a ticket inspector was approaching and I signalled to him for assistance as I threw open the compartment door.

James quickly shifted his feet and arms into a defensive position until he recognized me. Then he stood straight as the railway representative and I stepped into the room.

"What the devil is going on here, James," I demanded. Turning to the young lady I asked, "Are you all right, Miss Clemens?"

She nodded and James answered, "I am returning home, as I mentioned to you and Mr. Holmes the other day. Miss Clemens came by and asked to share my compartment. She stated she was going to Bristol on business for her father and would like some company for the trip.

"I certainly did not object. It is a long journey and as a gentleman I could not refuse a request that would leave a lady to herself in a foreign country."

Before he could continue, Miss Clemens shouted, "He's the thief who stole my father's papers, Doctor! Search his luggage and I'm sure you'll find them."

Taken aback by this remark I decided that it was time for Holmes involvement. I requested the inspector to fetch him from our compartment. I bade the young man to sit down opposite the author's daughter, while I remained standing in the doorway, in case I needed to act.

The inspector, whose name was Prentice, returned quickly with Holmes. I moved to the far side of the room with my back to the exterior windows where the countryside was sliding by at a brisk pace. Holmes now stood in the doorway I had vacated and took in the scene with his steel grey eyes.

James met his gaze without a flinch while Jean Clemens' face seemed to falter between anger and pleading.

Finally, Holmes spoke, "Miss Clemens, I am told you have accused Mr. James of theft. What, may I ask, has led you to that conclusion ?"

To his credit, the young man sat quietly, acquiescing to Holmes command at the moment.

The lady pointed at him and declared, "He arrived at the Langham the day after we did, Mr. Holmes, and became quite friendly with us. We often shared the elevator, I guess you call it the lift. So often in fact, it seemed more than coincidental. Through his conversations with us he knew of my father's papers and he was aware of our plans that night. Search his luggage – he must have the papers!" she demanded.

Holmes took in her statement and pondered it momentarily, then turned to the accused, "Mr. James, I am not a policeman, I have no authority to compel you to submit to such a search. However, as we still have several hours journey ahead, might it not be prudent to put an end to this dispute?"

Before he could answer, Prentice spoke up from the aisle way. "I have the authority, Mr. Holmes. Young man," he continued as he thrust out his hand, "your luggage ticket if you please."

James looked in turn to each of us and finally shrugged his shoulders and reached into his inner coat pocket. He handed over the stub and the inspector, exuding his authority, insisted that we all accompany him to the guard's van.

Once there we quickly found the two suitcases being transported by James and the inspector commanded him to unlock them. When he had done so, the railway man invited Sherlock Holmes to inspect them.

We all watched, Miss Clemens most eagerly of all, as Holmes methodically prodded through the garments and other items packed away. He examined the cases themselves for false compartments and at last turned toward the young lady.

"Miss Clemens, I am sorry, but your father's papers are not here. I am afraid you are mistaken."

She stared at Holmes, seemingly uncomprehending at first, then she glared at James, "No !" she shouted, it *must* be him !" Suddenly she pulled something from her purse and pointed it at the target of her accusations. "Tell me where they are !" she screamed.

To me the object appeared to be a ladies' compact, but suddenly Ward James was hitting me from the side with a tackle and a shout, "Look out, Doctor !"

We fell to the floor and she pointed the object again in our direction when Holmes brought his cane down upon her forearm and she dropped it as she screamed in pain from the blow.

There was a loud report, like that of a small caliber pistol. Prentice scooped the compact up. Suddenly Miss Clemens went into convulsions, and began to collapse. James rolled off of me and cushioned her fall before she hit the hard surface of the car.

She was shaking uncontrollably as I shuffled over to her on my knees. "She appears to be having an epilepsy attack," I cried. "Holmes, I need my medical bag, it's under the seat in our compartment!"

"I'll go!" shouted Prentice as he handed the compact to the detective and sprinted back toward the passenger car.

In the meantime, I pulled a handkerchief from my pocket and quickly rolled it up and placed it between the woman's teeth.

"I need to keep her from biting her tongue – aaggh!" I cried out as her jaws clamped down on my fingers.

James knelt by her head and pulled a cigar tube from his pocket. Gently he pried her mouth open to release my fingers and substituted the tube, making sure the handkerchief provided some cushion against her bite to prevent her breaking her teeth.

Holmes meantime, had procured a blanket to cover her and stuffed a rolled up nightshirt from James' luggage under her head as a pillow to keep her thrashing from resulting in a concussion against the hardwood floorboards.

Prentice quickly returned, panting from his efforts and handed me my bag. I administered what medications I had and eventually her convulsions subsided.

"Where's the nearest hospital ?" I enquired of the railway man who checked his watch.

"We're just about to come into Reading," he replied. "The Royal Berkshire Hospital is less than a mile from the station."

I turned to my companion, "Holmes, I must take her there and see to her care. You go on ahead and I'll catch up when I'm sure she's safe."

"Of course, Doctor," he replied.

Within a few minutes we slowed to a stop at Reading Station and Prentice arranged for an ambulance to transport us to the hospital. The medicine I had given Miss Clemens had helped her to sleep and thus she was in no condition to protest our actions. I climbed in beside her and turned back to my companion.

"Where will I find you in Bristol ?" I asked

"You will be able to contact me via telegraph through the Hippodrome Theatre," he replied. "Once I have arranged accommodations, I will wire you in care of the hospital and let you know where I am staying."

Ward James had assisted in conveying Miss Clemens to the ambulance and spoke up at this juncture, "You'd be welcome to stay at Roseboro, Mr. Holmes. I'm sure my father would enjoy meeting you."

"I will be out and about quite a bit, and at all hours, Mr. James," the detective replied, "I would not wish to disrupt the Earl's household."

"Visitors at Roseboro are constantly coming and going, Mr. Holmes, it would be no trouble at all" responded the young man.

Holmes gave a furtive glance toward me and nodded, "Very well, then. Watson, you may find me at Roseboro when you have completed your duties to your patient."

He closed the ambulance door and I found myself en route to the hospital, wondering at this turn of events and what Bristol would hold for my friend.

Chapter Eighteen

The Royal Berkshire Hospital in Reading was opened in 1839 on the London Road, on land donated by Henry Addington, the 1st Viscount Sidmouth, a Reading resident and former Prime Minister. The hospital was built by local architect and builder Henry Briant, winner of the design competition. The entrance is centred under a portico supported by six large fluted columns. King William IV took a keen interest in the hospital before it was built, and as a consequence his coat of arms appears on the central pediment, above this portico. Unfortunately his death preceded the facility's opening. Thus, the first patron of the hospital was William's niece and successor, Queen Victoria.

Upon our arrival, I informed the doctors on duty what had occurred and what medications I had administered so that they could proceed accordingly. I then sent a wire off to Jean's parents at the Langham to inform them of her condition and whereabouts. I received a reply within an hour, informing me that they would arrive via the Express train the next morning.

Deciding that I would await their arrival before proceeding on to re-join Holmes, I enquired of the medical staff of nearby accommodations where I could spend the night and be on call should my services be required. I was directed to a quiet inn just a short walk away, called the Knightly Lodgings.

As I entered the lobby of this establishment I was greeted warmly by a kindly faced woman of middle age, with blonde hair just starting to show streaks of grey.

"Good evening, Doctor," she called. "How long will ye be needin' to stay with us?"

At first her recognition of my occupation took me aback and I hesitantly replied "Most likely just for the night, Mrs ..."

"Raper, Nancy Raper. I'm the owner, and head chef, mind ye. Dinner will be served at seven so yer just in time and the kitchen closes at ten. Breakfast will be ready at seven-thirty. Are ye here with a patient at the Berkshire?"

By now I realized that she had noticed my medical bag in one hand, balancing off my suitcase in the other.

"Yes, my name is Watson. A young woman took ill on the train from London and I've checked her in until her parents arrive tomorrow."

"Well, that's a kindly thing for ye to set aside yer own plans to help out a fellow passenger. We get lots of visitin' doctors here, bein' so close by the hospital, but we've got a couple of rooms available right now. Let's see," she said, consulting her ledger, "We'll put ye in Number 6. That's at the back away from the road, just down that hallway," she pointed. "That way ye won't have to climb the stairs with yer leg."

Having luggage in both hands had precluded me from using my cane, which I clutched in tandem with the handle of my medical bag. The cold weather, plus my encounter with the baggage car floor, had set my old war wound to throbbing and no doubt she noticed my limp.

"You are quite observant, as well as accommodating, Mrs. Raper," I replied. "Thank you for your consideration."

"A lesson learned from my late husband, God rest his soul: always make your guests feel at home and your business will grow like a family."

"Sound advice," I smiled in agreement.

She retrieved a key and bid me follow her down the hallway.

"Normally my son, Robert, would be around to help you with your luggage, but he's not home from his job yet. I expect him along for dinner – he's always on time for that!" she laughed.

"What does he do?" I asked

"Oh, he's got a sharp mind, that one. Always experimentin' with the latest gadgets. He's got himself a job as an automobile mechanic. Says it's the next big industry and that we'll all be drivin' those rattlin' contraptions someday. He's got one himself, so you'll likely hear him when he gets here. Me, I'll take a reliable horse and trap any day."

As if on cue, the sound of a combustion engine insinuated itself, just as Mrs. Raper opened the door to my room.

"Ah, there be the lad now," she remarked. "Go ahead and settle in, Dr. Watson. Dinner will be a few more minutes."

She bustled off to her kitchen and I hung up those articles that needed hanging, found the washroom and presented myself in the dining room in less than fifteen minutes.

It was here I met my fellow lodgers. Two were visiting physicians and a third man was a construction engineer.

We all sat at table introducing ourselves as young Robert joined us, after helping his mother bring in the food. He was a lean young man of about my height, with the forearms of an ostler and the long fingers of a pianist. His brown unruly hair topped a pleasant round face from which two keen eyes seemed to take in all about him. I enquired whether his mother would be joining us.

"No, sir" he replied. "Mum has a rule that she doesn't eat until the guests have all been fed. She likes to keep herself available in case anyone needs anything else to go with their meal."

"Commendable," said Dr. Olin, an orthopaedic specialist who was about thirty-five years of age, with curly black hair and moustache. "Rare to find that in these smaller establishments. I'll wager you get your share of repeat business, young man."

"Yes, sir, we do seem to get the same folks coming back, especially doctors," answered Robert.

"Tell me, Dr. Watson, "asked the other physician, Dr. Van Dyke, a tall, thin man of about fifty. Though balding, he wore a brown beard and moustache indicative of his name, "What is your specialism?"

"I am a general practitioner, sir," I answered. "I was in Her Majesty's Service as an army surgeon with the Fifth Northumberland Fusiliers, before serving with the Berkshires at the battle of Maiwand. Since my return to civilian life I've been primarily a consulting physician with a small practice in London."

"Wait a minute," said young Robert. "Are you Dr. John Watson, the writer of the Sherlock Holmes stories?"

Modestly, I lowered my head as I cut into a delicious looking steak, "That was some years ago but yes, I am he."

"Unbelievable !" he cried, "What brings you to Reading ? Are you and Holmes on a case? Why haven't you written more about him?"

His questions came fast and furious and the excitement in his voice brought his mother from the kitchen.

"Robert, mind your manners!" she exclaimed. "The good doctor's business is none of yours."

"But, Mum ..."

"Enough! Eat your dinner and let the gentlemen enjoy their meal in peace."

"Yes, Mum," he replied, looking so dejected, I could not help but give him at least some measure of satisfaction to his curiosity.

"Sherlock Holmes is still quite active, though many of our cases deal with governments or private citizens who do not wish their names bandied about. He has also asked that I refrain from publishing, as he was getting too many requests regarding cases better handled by the police. He prefers to concentrate on the unusual or complex situations that give exercise to his intellect."

Van Dyke then asked, "What brings you to Reading then? Are you on a case now?"

"Holmes and I were on our way to Bristol, when a young lady of our acquaintance took ill on the train. He has gone on ahead while I see to her care here."

"What seems to be the matter with her?" he enquired.

"It appears to be some sort of epileptic fit." I replied. "It came on while she was extremely agitated."

"I have some experience in nervous conditions; perhaps I can be of assistance."

"That's most generous of you, sir," I responded. "I will be returning to the hospital after breakfast tomorrow; perhaps you can check on her with me then."

"Gladly, Doctor. I have a patient of my own to look in on and would be happy to accompany you."

The conversation lulled for a few moments as we continued to eat, one of those awkward situations where a room suddenly goes silent all at once. This was eventually broken by Mr. Brady, the construction engineer, a stocky, clean-shaven fellow in his late thirties.

"Tell me, master Robert, just how fast can that automobile of yours go?"

Glad to expound on his specialist area, the young man replied happily, "I've had her up to almost 20 miles an hour, I would guess. I've learned a lot from the other automobiles I've been working on and made some improvements to my own."

"That's amazing," replied Brady. "How do you find the roads between London and Bristol for travel by motorcar?"

"Well, sir, the Macadam portions are just fine. It's the stretches where it's still dirt that can be a problem, especially when the weather's bad. The ruts can be dangerous. But then, when the paved roads are wet, the tires just don't have the traction, or the sense of a good horse, to stop very fast."

We all laughed at that. Then I asked Brady what type of construction he had been working on recently.

"To tell the truth, Dr. Watson, I've been primarily involved in bridges and tunnels, but I've just taken an assignment to scout out the roads between London and Bristol for a competitor in the 1000 mile automobile trial coming up in April."

"Really?" responded Robert. "I hadn't heard about that."

"Oh it's going to be quite exciting," responded the engineer, "It's the idea of Claude Johnson, Secretary of the

Automobile Club.[1] They're going to drive as many vehicles as possible from London to Edinburgh and back to prove the performance and reliability of these new motorcars. We already have over fifty entries from all sorts of folks."

"So, is it a race then?" I enquired

"Actually, it's more of an endurance test, Doctor. The speed limit has been set at 12 miles per hour and only eight when going through towns and villages. The idea is that they will stop at several cities and allow people to view the automobiles and ask questions. Sort of a combination of publicity and advertising, as well as swaying public opinion toward being more accepting of this new mode of transportation."

"What kind of vehicles are allowed?" prodded Robert. "Could I enter my Daimler?"

"Oh, certainly that would be allowed," replied Brady. "We've already accepted Daimlers, Benz, Panhard, Napier, Peugeot and a Darracq."

The conversation continued on in this vein as we completed our meal. After dinner, we opted to venture out to the stable with our cigars and let Robert show us his motorcar. It was a Daimler, with a twin-cylinder six horsepower engine, mounted at the front of the vehicle. It had a four-speed gearbox and chain drive and was manufactured in 1897. Daimler built them in Coventry, 100 miles north of Reading. Somehow this particular automobile had overturned in an accident nearby and was given up by its owner, who sold it for scrap to Robert's employer. The boy had arranged to work extra hours to be able to buy it. He spent all his spare time fixing and refining it, which accounted for his lateness in coming home.

In appearance, it reminded me of pictures I had seen of the Conestoga wagons that crossed the Great Plains of the United States on their way west. It was much shorter of course, but it sat high on large, spoke wheels, very much like wagon wheels, but with rubber tyres wrapped around them. It used a

---

[1] Forerunner of the Royal Automobile Club. Eventually 83 vehicles would join this tour.

tiller rather than the steering wheel arrangement that was becoming popular with so many vehicles.

"You seem to have excellent ground clearance," noted Brady. "I can't imagine that ruts would be much of a problem from that aspect."

"It's not the clearance that's ever given me trouble," replied the young enthusiast. "It's the fact that the wheels are so narrow that if they get into a deep rut it takes quite a bit of effort to get them out again. With the power of the engine behind the weight of the car it can bend or break a wheel under some conditions."

The engineer took a closer look and nodded, "Yes I can see where that might be an issue. It appears that a wider wheel might better serve the overall design."

"That's been my thought," replied Robert. "But no one is making anything as wide as I'm thinking it needs to be. I'd make them myself but then where would I get tyres to fit?"

By this point, we doctors were feeling left out of the discussion and returned to the house while the engineer and the mechanic continued on with their discussion.

After a delicious dessert of cheesecake and coffee we each retired to our rooms. I proceeded to read a newspaper I had picked up en route and eventually tired my eyes enough to retreat to clean sheets and warm blankets for a good night's rest.

Chapter Nineteen

The next morning found me and my fellow lodgers enjoying a hearty breakfast of bacon, sausage and eggs, as we prepared to journey on to our patients. Just as the two doctors and I exited the establishment, young Robert was cranking up the engine on his Daimler. We watched in fascination. When he got it going he called out to us,

"Can I give you a ride, doctors? It's right on my way to work."

We accepted his offer and climbed aboard. In less than five minutes we found ourselves at the hospital entrance waving goodbye to our young friend as he sped off to his job.

"What do you think, Watson?" enquired Dr. Olin as we walked into the hospital, "Will those things really become the normal mode of transportation for the masses?"

"I don't know about the masses," I replied, "but I can imagine that, as they improve and become more reliable, they will be a great boon to police, fire and ambulance services. Can you imagine in the not too distant future, as telephone coverage becomes more widespread, people will be able to call for your services as a doctor and you can use your automobile to speed to their door? Perhaps in time to save a life."

"Yes, I can see that," interjected Van Dyke. "However, it will require a great deal of work on the part of the government to improve the country's roads."

"I suppose that's part of the reason for this 1000 mile trial." I responded. "If enough people get behind a cause, who knows what can happen?"

While Olin left us to attend the orthopedic ward, Van Dyke and I proceeded upstairs to the first floor where Miss Clemens was currently confined to a private room. We met

Dr. Newcombe, one of the resident physicians, who informed us my patient had spent a quiet night with no further convulsions. She was demure and almost apologetic when she awoke early that morning.

"She seems quite the normal young lady today, Dr. Watson. It seems the crisis has passed, but I would like to get more history on her."

I checked my watch, "Her parents are coming in on the morning Express. They should be here within the next hour or so."

"Very good," he responded. "She is quite alert if you would like to see her now. I would imagine she would welcome a familiar face."

"Of course," I replied and Van Dyke and I proceeded to her room where we found her sitting up and just finishing her breakfast.

She immediately became animated upon recognizing me. "Dr. Watson!" she cried, "I am so glad to see you!"

I put down my bag and took her outstretched hand in both my own and gazed into her now shining and alert eyes.

"I am glad to see you so much better, Miss Clemens," I replied. Taking my right hand from her grasp I felt her forehead which was quite normal.

"How are you feeling?" I continued.

"Just a little weak, Doctor, I'm sure I'll be fine and please, call me Jean."

"Very well, Jean. This is Dr. Van Dyke. He's a specialist and would like to take a look at you."

Her hand squeezed mine in apprehension, betraying her feelings despite the calmness in her voice.

"You will stay, won't you?"

"Of course, Jean, I'll be right here."

"All right, thank you," she acquiesced, letting go of my hand.

I stepped aside and allowed Dr. Van Dyke to begin his examination. He was quite thorough, checking her eyes, ears, pulse, heart, lungs and reflexes. He asked her numerous questions and finally seemed satisfied.

"Well young lady, you seem quite fine now. I believe this episode has passed. You should be up and about by tomorrow as long as you eat well and drink plenty of fluids today."

Turning to me so that she could not see his face, he mouthed silently, "I will talk to you later." Out loud he merely stated, "Dr. Watson, I have another patient to see. If you could inform me when her parents arrive I do have some questions for them."

"Of course," I replied.

He left us alone and I sat down next to her bed.

"Well that wasn't so bad was it?" I stated calmly.

"No, I suppose not," she replied. "I just hate it when these things happen, especially when I can't remember it all."

"What do you recall?" I asked.

She closed her eyes briefly then opened them and looked at me, "I remember confronting Mr. James in his compartment and then you and Mr. Holmes and the conductor taking us back to the baggage car to check his luggage."

She stopped and pressed her palms to her eyes, "I was so sure he must have Papa's papers."

"Holmes was quite thorough in his search," I said.

"And that's all I can remember," she continued, suddenly rubbing her jaw which would be sore from the muscles clenching as they did.

She looked at me, "What happened?"

I weighed my options at this juncture, uncertain as to how much I should reveal for fear of triggering another attack.

Opting on the side of caution I answered without details, "You became very upset. I believe your disappointment caused your blood pressure to rise and set off this convulsion that caused you to lose consciousness."

She took in that statement and then asked, "Did someone get hurt? I seem to remember a loud noise."

'No, no one was injured. In fact, Mr. James caught you before you hit the floor when you fainted."

She bunched up her blanket under her chin and briefly bit her thumb in contemplation. "He does seem a nice man," she said. "But he also knew everything the thief would need to know and his room *is* just down the hall."

"Yes," I replied, "But he left the hotel at seven o'clock and was gone for the evening as well. He has witnesses proving that he did not return until well after eleven. Besides, he is the son of an Earl, what use could he possibly have for your father's papers?"

"Oh you English and your titles," she sighed in exasperation. "After all that you've written about Mr. Holmes' cases, surely you recognize that criminality does not restrict itself to the lower classes."

"Of course," I agreed. "However crime generally has a motive, and none seem to exist that would implicate Mr. James."

"No, I suppose not," she reluctantly agreed. "But then why were you and Mr. Holmes going to Bristol?"

"We are following a lead on another suspect who was staying at the hotel. An actor, who may have at least some use for your father's works."

"Really?" she brightened.

"Do not raise your hopes yet, Jean. But have no fear either. If anyone can track your father's burglar it is Sherlock Holmes."

At that moment a nurse entered, announcing it was time for her patient's sponge bath, so I slipped out assuring the young lady that I would return when her parents arrived.

I returned to the lobby on the ground floor and informed the desk I would be in the hospital library and to please inform me when Mr. Clemens and his wife arrived.

Shortly after I had settled in with a medical journal, Dr. Van Dyke found me and sat down to discuss his prognosis.

"I need to consult some journals, Watson and talk to her parents to get some more history, but I believe we have a rather aggressive case of epilepsy in this young woman."

"I've only been in her presence a few times," I replied. "This is the first time I've seen any sign of her condition."

"It may be a new development or it may occur only in certain situations, such as the agitation you mentioned. What were the circumstances exactly?"

Without revealing names, I explained how she had accused a young man of a theft against her father. Then, when Holmes proved that the fellow did not have the items in question, she became even more agitated and convulsed.

"I see," he responded thoughtfully, stroking his beard absent-mindedly as he pondered this information. "There could be some psychological aspects to her condition. Hopefully, an interview with her parents will provide some clues for a more thorough diagnosis."

We went on to discuss his other case while waiting for the Clemens' arrival. When a page informed us they were here, we met them in the lobby and took them immediately to Jean's room.

The family reunion was quite emotional. Jean was apologetic, Olivia was in tears over her daughter's plight and Clemens, himself, was quite moved and uncharacteristically silent.

Dr. Newcombe informed them that, barring any relapse, Jean would be able to leave the hospital the next day. That brought a great sense of relief to all. After a time, it was decided that the young lady should rest and the Clemens, Dr. Van Dyke and I adjourned to the hospital library where we could further discuss her case.

As it turned out, Jean had a history of epilepsy from the time she was fifteen, which her father attributed to a head injury she had suffered at the age eight or nine. The family had spent years seeking cures in the United States and Europe. Clemens also attributed her mood swings and sometimes erratic behavior to her uncontrolled epilepsy.

"What was she doing on that train?" he asked.

"Apparently she was quite convinced that Ward James was the thief who stole your papers," I replied. "She confronted him and when the ticket inspector allowed Holmes to search his luggage to no avail, she became extremely agitated and went into her convulsion."

"She ... she didn't hurt anyone did she?" asked Olivia Clemens, hesitantly, with a mother's fear in her voice.

"Oh no, no," I answered. "She did pull some kind of weapon, but Holmes disarmed her before anyone was injured."

"Oh my God!" Olivia cried, burying her face in her kerchief as the tears flowed.

Clemens spoke up at that, as he put a comforting hand on his wife's shoulder, "We've taken weapons away from her before," he recalled. "We want her to be able to protect herself, but when she has one of her spells it's too dangerous."

"Well, she is unarmed now," I replied. "Holmes has the weapon, some kind of pistol I believe, and we can return it to you when we get back to London."

"Oh, you just keep it, Doc," responded the author. "No sense puttin' temptation in her hands again."

Van Dyke continued with some questions of his own and agreed to follow up with them in a few days, after they had all returned to London.

I suggested that Mr. And Mrs. Clemens should come to the Knightly Lodgings with me so they could arrange accommodations until they could take their daughter back to the Langham. They readily agreed. We took the short walk as I helped the elderly gentleman carry their bags, so Olivia could tread the path unburdened.

When we arrived at Mrs. Raper's establishment she was quite sympathetic and fixed them up with a room immediately. I told her that I would be catching the evening train to Bristol and would be checking out late that afternoon.

While Olivia Clemens rested in her room Sam and I braved the coolness of the day to smoke out on the front porch. Being outside, and making sure I was upwind, I was protected from the odour of his cigar. The sky was filled with high, light grey clouds that kept the winter temperature low, but were not threatening to shed their watery contents upon us as yet.

Our discussion turned toward a literary nature. We debated the merits of first person accounts versus third person narratives. Huckleberry Finn being an example of the first while Tom Sawyer, the latter.

Of course, my own preference had always been that of the first person account. I felt I could relate Holmes' adventures much better in that fashion. However, Clemens was quite convincing about some of the aspects of story-telling which can be lost by that method.

We were thus engaged when Robert came chugging up in his motorcar and stopped in front of us. He dismounted from his high perch and pushed his driving goggles high up on his forehead, actually pushing his cap back somewhat to accommodate their diameter.

"Hello, Dr. Watson," he called. "How's your patient ?"

"Just fine, Robert. I'll be off to join Holmes in Bristol on the train later. By the way," I turned to my companion, "this is Samuel Clemens."

Robert shook his hand without recognition of the name, "Pleased to meet you, sir."

He then turned back to me. "Say, Dr. Watson, my boss has asked me to drive into Bristol for some parts he needs. I'm going to be heading out right after lunch. I can get you there long before the evening train."

Eager to re-join my friend, I accepted his generous offer. We had some little time before lunch and so I excused myself from Clemens' company and went to pack my bag, leaving him in the company of the young mechanic.

As I was doing so, a telegram, re-directed from the hospital, arrived to inform me where to meet Holmes that night. Assuming I would be on the evening train, Holmes had directed me to join him at the Hippodrome and informed me that a ticket would be waiting for me at the box office.

Of course, were I going by train, my arrival would have been around the time of intermission. I had the messenger follow me out to the porch where I questioned Robert.

"What time would you say we'll be arriving in Bristol, Robert?"

"Well, if the weather holds, we should get there around six or six-thirty," he replied.

I wrote this down as a reply to Holmes, informing him I should be there for the start of the performance. I paid the messenger and he pedaled off on his bicycle with my answer, enviously eyeing the automobile parked in front of the porch.

Clemens, himself, was taking a closer look at it, clucking his tongue and shaking his head in wonder. "Back when I was a riverboat pilot, some 40 years ago mind you, I sometimes wondered if the steam engine that drove those big paddle wheels could ever be compacted enough to drive a wagon. After all," he continued, "it's no different than drivin' a train, 'ceptin' you don't need any tracks!

"Now here they come along and invent a whole new infernal combustion engine that can fit in a vehicle small enough to travel the highways and byways. Makes you wonder what the next 40 years'll bring along."

"We do live in a marvellous age, Sam," I replied. "With the harnessing of electricity, the invention of the telephone, improvements to all sorts of appliances and gadgets, advances in medicine … why we've probably come farther in the past 40 years than in the last thousand before that."

"That reminds me of my story about Hank Morgan," he responded, "using his 19th century knowledge to baffle and amaze the folks in 6th century England and set old Merlin to shakin' in his boots."[1]

"Really ?" piped up Robert, "I've never heard of that story and I thought I knew all the legends about King Arthur."

"Well," answered Clemens, "that's the thing about legends. When there are little to no facts to be contradicted, a soul can make up just about anything and add it on to the story. When I get back to London I'll send you a copy."

Robert thanked the aging writer, still unaware, I'm sure, as to whom he was speaking. At that moment his mother called us in to lunch and we all sat down to an excellent meal.

---

[1] *A Connecticut Yankee in Kings Arthur's Court.* Published in 1889

Chapter Twenty

"Mrs. Raper," I exclaimed, when finished stuffing myself once again, "you are an absolutely marvellous cook. I shall certainly insist that Holmes and I stay here whenever a case brings us this way again."

"That's mighty kind of ye, Doctor," she replied. "Don't forget to tell yer friends."

"I shall indeed, madam," I replied as I finished my coffee. Turning to her son I asked, "Well, Robert are we ready to go?"

We bundled my luggage into the car and Mrs. Raper was kind enough to provide me with a pillow for a seat cushion and some travelling rugs to stem the cold.

"Ye come back and see us again sometime, Dr. Watson," she called as Robert cranked up the motor. I assured her I would do so and off we sped, along London Road and Berkeley Avenue towards the Bath Road, the main route westward.

Robert had modified this particular Daimler and added an enclosure he had salvaged from an old growler cab. Thus, we had a roof over our heads and protection against side winds. There was no windshield, so plenty of cold air blew in as we chugged along the road and I was grateful for my heavy overcoat, scarf, gloves and the rugs for my legs.

My companion, with the exuberance of youth, seemed to take no notice of the weather. He was certainly dressed warmly with a heavy Ulster coat, dark grey in colour, which helped to detract from its grease and oil stains. He also wore leather gloves, flat cap and goggles. However, he used no rug for his legs, preferring to keep them free to operate the vehicle. The noise of the motor and the wind created by our speed discouraged conversation, so I settled back and read a paper I had picked up at the hospital.

At one point, after we had passed beyond Theale and were moving in a southwesterly direction toward Woolhampton through acres of farmland, the young man opened the throttle all the way. Outside of a train with its cosy comforts, I had never experienced such speed. In the small confines of the automobile, with wide open space around us, it was quite exhilarating. I leaned forward and spoke loudly towards his ear.

"How fast are we going?"

He glanced down at some gages and replied, "We're up to 18 miles per hour, Doctor."

"Does the greater speed affect how fast the petrol is used up?" I enquired, not knowing when or where he planned to refuel.

"Oh, we'll be fine. There's a place in Newbury where I can fill up again. We should be there in less than an hour."

I settled back into my seat. Fortunately this stretch of our journey was on a macadam roadway. The smoother asphalt surface allowed me to continue my reading for a time. However, I finished the paper long before we arrived at Newbury. Not having the option to nap that a train may afford, I took out my notes regarding our case to see what avenues might present themselves to me regarding Clemens' culprit.

Looking over the list of guests who may have had access to Clemens' room, I attempted to construct a timeline based upon what we had been told regarding the whereabouts of each.

Sam had told us that they were gone from six o'clock until "nearly midnight". That left the possibility of six hours for the thief to do his work, assuming, of course, that he did not attempt his burglary while the family slept.

Adelaide and her children, though I could not consider them suspects, left at six-twenty and saw no one in the hall, but noticed Hodges' boots by the front of his door.

John Clay left his room at four-thirty and returned at six-thirty, purportedly in for the evening. His valet, Gilliam, was out from four-thirty until eleven and Holmes had confirmed his alibi at the billiards club. Clay, if telling the truth, heard a noise "before eight o'clock" out on his balcony. That could have been the case being lowered to the alley.

Hodges, whose boots matched the prints in Clemens' room, was supposedly out from six o'clock until seven-thirty. His brown boots were in the hallway when he left and still there upon his return. According to the hotel bootblack, those boots were damp on the bottom when he picked them up at one in the morning.

Ward James was gone from seven o'clock until midnight. Sir Edwin Snider had vouched for his dinner with James to Hopkins. Holmes had confirmed the young man's presence at the Sanford House for the latter part of the evening.

The Robinsons were an unlikely pair of thieves. They had admitted to being in all night, having ordered room service. This certainly would have given them opportunity to sneak down to Clemens' room. However, the young bride's apprehension at burglary seemed genuine. As I thought this through, however, they did elope without parental permission, according to Constable Keyzers, which would certainly put Robinson's job in jeopardy. The theft of Clemens' papers could result in a monetary profit for him through sale or ransom. Yet this burglary seemed to require more planning than a chance meeting up with the Clemens clan at the Langham. Robinson had worked steadily up in Manchester until his elopement. It was unlikely that he would have known of Clemens' plans, or that the author carried about such valuable papers.

At this juncture I was still not convinced that Clay was not involved. I admit his arrogance, conceit and reputation prompted me to a natural dislike for the man. Even setting aside those feelings, his past still reeked of actions that would make this crime seem a natural act for him.

Then again, Hodges was also in the vicinity, his boot tracks were in the room and as an employee for a competing publisher, one who might harbour ill feelings against Clemens, he seemed to have the most plausible motive.

Yet there was still this Smith fellow, whom Holmes was tracking down. His occupation as an actor could give him a motive for the theft, either for his own use or to sell to some fellow thespian. There were some bits of cloth stuck on the fire escape railing outside Clemens' rooms. While Holmes considered them planted, it didn't mean that Smith couldn't have planted them, since they were on the downward rail and he would have come from above. How obvious would it be for him to try and misdirect investigators into the opposite direction from which he came?

Suddenly, my thoughts were disrupted by a sharp turning of the vehicle and a swerving back into line. I found myself thrown off balance and down onto one knee, fortunately on my good leg.

"Sorry, Doctor," said Robert, as I hauled myself back up into my seat, "Couldn't take a chance on hitting that deer."

I picked up my notes and replied, "I'm afraid I wasn't paying attention or I would have braced myself better."

"It's a bit of a problem with wild game crossing the roads," he stated. "They aren't used to anything this big moving this fast and sometimes they just freeze and stare, especially deer. It would cripple us for sure to have a couple hundred pounds of venison indenting the engine compartment."

"Well, I commend your reactions," I replied. Looking about the countryside slipping so quickly by us I asked, "Whereabouts are we?"

"We passed Woolhampton while you were writing, I didn't want to disturb you so I didn't mention it. That's Thatcham up ahead and Newbury lies just beyond that."

I could see some buildings just ahead and a haze of smoke from scores of chimneys hung above the town. Robert slowed our speed considerably and we passed through at about the pace of a carriage horse at a good steady trot.

Nearly everyone on the streets stopped to stare at us, being, no doubt, unused to seeing a motorcar, especially one that had been so customized as this. Many waved and children and dogs chased after us.

"Do you get this sort of reaction often?" I asked.

"Pretty much whenever I leave Reading," he replied. "The folks there are used to seeing me, but it's still pretty new when I get out to other towns."

Upon leaving Thatcham, we quickly came upon Newbury in less than two miles. Robert found the business where he could fill up the fuel tank. I admit the smell of the petrol was both, intoxicating and nauseating, a unique combination in my experience.

When he went to pay the proprietor for the fuel, he found himself rewarded with a proposition. The gentleman, by the name of Roebuck, a big strong man of blacksmith proportions, offered him half price if Robert would pick up a cargo box for him from the docks at Avonmouth, just northwest of Bristol, where ships came up the Bristol channel to unload their goods. They measured the interior of the Daimler and determined that the box would fit behind the driver's seat, assuming that I was no longer riding back there.

With the bargain struck and our having used the facilities and purchased some refreshment to drink along the way, we departed once again on our westward journey.

"How often will we have to stop for fuel?" I asked.

"I've got two five gallon cans of petrol in the boot, but we should be able to make it to Bristol easily on what I have in the tank now," he replied. "I just like to be safe and make sure I'm never so low on fuel that I can't get to the next supply."[1]

"Then there will be no more stops along the way?" I enquired.

"Oh, we'll stop a few more times just to stretch our legs and let the tyres and the engine cool down a bit. But we're making good time; if I can let the engine run full out in between towns we'll easily be in Bristol by six o'clock."

"Excellent!" I replied as I sat back in my seat. I had already missed what Holmes was hoping would be his encounter with A.W. Smith the previous evening. I was anxious to catch up to my friend and see where matters now stood in our case.

---

[1] The 1897 Coventry Daimler could travel roughly 100 km (62 miles) on 6.5 gallons

Chapter Twenty-One

I feel I must backtrack at this juncture and bring the reader up to date regarding the events Holmes was experiencing while I had been tending to my patient. Not being an eyewitness to these incidents, I naturally had to rely upon Holmes' later recollection. This can be somewhat problematic, in that his reports are very, shall I say 'sterile'. They tend to relate only to the facts he deems relevant to his deductive reasoning. They are quite concise, no doubt. However they tend to lack the descriptions which help to set the scenes of the action. I have had to rely on my own later observations of the surroundings to fully flesh out the occurrences. I beg the reader's indulgence and claim some measure of poetic license as to their accuracy.

After I had left them at Reading Station, Holmes and Ward James had continued on toward Bristol. Holmes declined James' invitation to join him in his compartment, preferring to ponder the facts of the case over a pipe or two in the solace of his own space.

Upon their arrival in Bristol, after many stops along the way, Holmes found the gentleman under a lamppost near the guard's van. James had procured a porter for his own luggage and Holmes was carrying his carpetbag, so they proceeded to the street side of the station. There a carriage from Roseboro was waiting for the young master of the house.

"Evenin', Master Ward," said the groom. "Have a nice trip, did ye now?"

"Yes, Johnny, all went well. Father will be pleased," he replied. Then he introduced Holmes.

"A great pleasure, sir," Johnny responded, with knuckles to forehead in a type of salute. "We received the

Young master's telegram from Reading and the housemaids have a room all prepared for ye. Lord Roseboro himself is most anxious to meet ye."

"If I may impose one request?" asked the detective, "Would it be possible to stop by the Hippodrome on the way to Roseboro ?"

The groom looked to his master who answered, "Certainly, Mr. Holmes, it's not far from here at all."

Climbing aboard the carriage, James pulled up a briefcase and handed it to my friend. "This was not amongst the luggage, Mr. Holmes, and I am afraid Miss Clemens did not notice it in the rack above my seat in our compartment. I insist that you take a look for yourself to allay any further suspicion."

Holmes could hardly help but accept the case that had been thrust nearly into his lap. "Your candour does you credit, sir," he responded.

After a cursory search that showed the papers within were documents related to the Earl's business, Holmes snapped the case shut and returned it to the owner.

"I'm sure Miss Clemens will be both happy for your honesty and sorry for her accusations," he stated.

"I just hope that she is all right. Will you be contacting Dr. Watson in Reading?"

"I shall send him a telegram in the morning."

"Please express my regrets," continued James, "I do hope that her recovery will be rapid."

"Watson is an excellent physician. If he cannot treat her himself he will certainly arrange for someone who is more specialized to do so. She is in good hands."

I confess that I was most gratified when Holmes later told me of his exchange – but to continue with my friend's account …

"What alerted you to the fact that Miss Clemens was holding a weapon?" asked Holmes, as he pulled the device from his coat pocket. "It certainly doesn't appear to be so at first glance."

James took the device from Holmes' hand and proceeded to study it, "Not when viewed like this, no. But from where I was standing all I could see was what appeared to be a gun barrel in her hand. She was shaking with such rage I feared the doctor's leg injury might not allow him to react in time to take cover."

Holmes took the device as he handed it back, "It is a unique weapon. A .32 calibre Chicago Firearms Company protector palm pistol, circa 1890, I believe. Its appearance makes it seem like a harmless ladies' compact, except for the barrel that protrudes between the fingers and this lever handle that acts as a trigger. It can fire seven-shots, one each time the handle is squeezed."

"Hardly an accurate weapon I would think," commented James.

"Certainly not something you would take target practice with," agreed Holmes as he put it back into his pocket. "However, it is meant as a short range protection device against footpads or anyone intent on assaulting the lady who carries it. For that purpose it is quite well suited."

"I'm just glad we did not experience the damage it could do first hand."

"Indeed," replied my friend. "Ah, I believe that is the Hippodrome."

Johnny pulled up in front of the theatre which was naturally dark, being closed on Mondays. "I'm afraid there's no one about," called Johnny as Holmes stepped down to the grey brick road.

"Possibly not," said Holmes, checking his watch, for by now it was nearly ten o'clock. "I'll just make a quick enquiry at the stage door, I shall return momentarily."

A knock on the stage door at the end of the passageway, which was to the left of the box office, was answered by an elderly gentleman, whose name I later discovered was Zachariah.

"Good evening, sir!" exclaimed Holmes in a jubilant fashion. "I am here on behalf of Sir Henry Irving. I've just arrived on the London train and was wondering if I was in time to catch an actor by the name of A.W. Smith?"

Zachariah took his pipe from between his clenched teeth, looked Holmes up and down, and replied, "A.W. Smith, you say, hmm. Oh, you must mean Arthur. Nope, all the actors finished rehearsin' 'bout half an hour ago. Won't be back 'til four, tomorrow afternoon."

Holmes feigned disappointment and sighed, "Very well, I shall return tomorrow."

As he turned to go, the old stage manager asked, "Any message?"

Holmes stopped and smiled back at him, "I would prefer to deliver my news in person, but thank you."

As he returned to James' carriage the young lord asked him, "Any luck?"

"The players have retired for the evening," replied the detective. "I shall have to pursue my investigation tomorrow."

"Well then," responded the heir to Roseboro, "let us be off to a late supper, a warm bed and a fresh start tomorrow.

They proceeded south, then west, passed Cannon's Marsh and down across the River Avon. Turning north into Clanage Road they passed Leigh Woods and within the hour, found themselves at Roseboro.

Holmes and his host were greeted at the door by the major domo, Rupert, who welcomed them both and took their coats. He was the typically efficient butler with just a trace of informality that, Holmes would later discover, permeated the household, a reflection of Lord Roseboro's down to earth personality. He was stocky and filled out his butlers' garb quite amply. Balding, with a fringe of white hair ringing his crown, he looked to be in his fifties. He had one of the servants take the luggage to their respective rooms and then informed James and Holmes that the Earl was awaiting them in the study.

The "study" was very large and more a library than any small town or village could boast. Hundreds of books filled the floor to ceiling shelves and a rolling ladder was necessary to access the upper shelves This particular room extended three floors as a balcony surrounded the top floor with egress to the upper floor rooms. A spiral staircase descended down on to the main floor where they stood.

There were several upholstered chairs and sofas scattered about, mostly in forest green and burgundy, in a variety of solids, stripes and patterns. The Earl rose from one of these with some little effort and assistance from an oak walking stick with a brass dog-head handle.

Harrison James, Earl of Roseboro by name, was in his late forties, about five foot seven inches tall and of medium build, tending toward a pot belly of middle age. He had medium length brown hair, parted down the middle, that was surprisingly free of grey, considering his full moustache and a short cropped beard had both nearly completely lost the colour of their youth.

He stood, with the assistance of the well-worn cane, for his left leg had been permanently injured some years before. Extending his hand, he welcomed Holmes heartily and then gave his son a pat on the shoulder. "All went well with Sir Edwin, I trust?"

"Yes, father," answered the dutiful son. "I think you will be quite pleased."

"Excellent!" he exclaimed, "But that can wait for the morning."

Turning to my friend he enquired, "Mr. Holmes, I cannot tell you how privileged I feel to have you as a guest in my home. I have followed your adventures with great interest. Not only those written by Dr. Watson, but what little which has appeared in the newspapers as well. Which is quite fortunate, for that is how we discovered that you had not perished at the Reichenbach Falls where Watson last wrote of you."

"Yes," replied the detective, taking the seat offered by the elder James and accepting a generous glass of burgundy as well. "I have tended to avoid unnecessary publicity these past few years, much to Watson's chagrin I imagine."

"He does weave a fine tale, Mr. Holmes, I'm sure the public would welcome more stories of your past cases. But, tell me, what brings you to our humble city? Surely London has not run its course of unsolved crimes and mysteries?"

"I'm afraid, your Lordship, London will never be crime free, so long as the human race inhabits its boundaries," answered Holmes, taking a sip of wine and smiling in appreciation at the vintage.

Continuing he said, "No, in this case a possible criminal has fled the limits of the capital and was last known to be coming here. I am merely following up on a hypothesis. That part of being a consulting detective is something that Watson generally fails to include in his narratives. They are so time-consuming and more often than not prove fruitless."

"You mean," interjected the younger James, smiling as he spoke, "that you don't really solve every crime within a week?"

"Hardly," Holmes smiled back. "They can be quite lengthy at times. Take Professor Moriarty, for example. It took years to gather enough conclusive evidence for Scotland Yard to obtain an arrest warrant."

"Well," responded the Earl, "anything we can do to help speed your task, you only have to ask. There will be a carriage and driver at your disposal in the morning and, should you need their help, I even have a bit of influence with the local magistrate and chief constable."

"You are most generous, Lord Roseboro," replied the famous sleuth. "I think a night's rest for now will be quite sufficient. I will do my best not to disrupt your household while I am here."

"Nonsense," replied the Earl, standing as Holmes finished his drink and also stood. "Rupert will show you to your room. If your schedule allows, we would be happy for you to breakfast with us at eight. My wife will be joining us and would love to meet you. Unfortunately, she has already retired for this evening, having put in a long day and being unprepared for a late night. However one of the grooms can be ready as early as you like, should you need to be off somewhere."

"Please allow them to sleep in, your Lordship. My only plans for the morning will be to send a telegram to Watson. After breakfast will be quite suitable for doing that. However, I may need their service well into the night."

"Very well, then, good night, Mr. Holmes," answered the Earl.

Holmes bade good night to his two hosts and followed the butler out to ascend two flights of the main staircase to a bedroom on the second floor.

*****

Come morning, Holmes arose early. The morning fog obscured any prediction of what weather may attend the day, so Holmes bundled himself up and took a stroll about the gardens. He smoked a small cherry-wood pipe and meandered among the vegetation as he pondered our case. He had wandered some couple of hundred yards from the main house and decided to circle back. Soon he found the path he had chosen delivered him to the stables and he opted to step inside.

He was immediately met by Johnny who, with several other ostlers and stable boys, was attending to the morning feeding of the horses. Two maids were milking cows.

"May I help ye, Mr. Holmes?" asked Johnny, eagerly.

Johnny was a young man, roughly the same age as Ward James. He was of slight build but strong for his size, for he was quite capable of handling any horse or team among the Roseboro stock. He had dark red wavy hair that sprang from beneath his flat cap in all directions like the snakes of Medusa. His freckled Irish face seemed to wear a perpetual grin beneath a handlebar moustache and bright, intelligent blue eyes.

"Thank you, no," replied the detective. "I'm just out for some morning air."

"Well, anything ye need, ye just ask," replied the groom. "We've al'ays got standin' orders to assist, Mr. Holmes."

"Always?" responded my friend, curiously.

"I'm sorry, Mr. Holmes," countered Johnny more slowly, with a bit of consternation on his face. "Sometimes me accent gets in the way o' me tongue. I mean 'all of us', got standin' orders to assist ye, sir."

"Ah, I see," replied Holmes, knocking out his pipe and stuffing it into his coat packet. "You may satisfy my curiosity on one point, Johnny," he continued.

"What might that be, sir ?"

"I noticed new construction on the far side of the stables. Is the Earl expanding his stock ?"

"Oh, no, sir, that is purely for the master. He's got his eye on one of them new automobile machines and wants a place to keep it out o' the weather, but away from the horses. He figures to build hisself a machine shop where he can work on it in peace without scarin' the livestock."

"A wise precaution," observed Holmes. After a pause he continued, "I shall need transportation to the nearest telegraph office after breakfast, Johnny. If you would please arrange that I shall be grateful."

"I'll drive ye meself, Mr. Holmes. I'll have a coach ready for ye whenever ye wish to leave."

"Thank you," replied Holmes and then he turned on his heel and made his way back to the main house.

Entering through the kitchen, Holmes was assaulted by a variety of savory odours that would tempt any man to overstuffing himself on their origins.

"Ye must be Mr. Holmes," called out a pleasant middle-aged woman with the same scarlet hair and Irish accent as Johnny. It proved no coincidence, as she introduced herself as his mother, Mrs. O'Reilly.

"Breakfast will be served in twenty minutes, but would ye like a cup o' tea, or some coffee perhaps?" she enquired, dutifully.

"I did not mean to disturb your kitchen routine, Mrs. O'Reilly," he answered, "However, some hot coffee would be quite welcome, as there is a bit of a chill outside."

"Aye," she replied as she poured a cup of strong black coffee., "There'll be rain by this afternoon, mark me words, I can feel it in me bones."

"Thank you," replied Holmes, intending the remark for both the coffee, as he gratefully accepted it from her, and the weather prediction, to which he replied with a smile, "I shall be sure to dress accordingly and take my umbrella."

"Ye'll be the wiser and drier for it, Mr. Holmes," she responded and then excused herself back to her stove while Holmes ventured on to the study.

There he found the Earl and his wife, engaged in conversation. He turned to leave, but was forestalled by his host, who greeted him with enthusiasm and introduced him to the Countess.

"Jenny, this is Mr. Sherlock Holmes, the famous detective from London. Mr. Holmes, my wife, Genevieve."

Holmes bowed over her extended hand as good manners dictate and responded, "*Enchante'*, Lady Roseboro. May I compliment you on your beautiful home."

"Thank you, Mr. Holmes," she replied, "I cannot take credit for its origins, but I do attempt to be a good caretaker of the work Harrison's parents left to us."

Lady Roseboro, née Genevieve Lefebvre, was an attractive woman in her late forties. Her chestnut brown hair showed not a streak of grey and was full and flowing well past her shoulders. She spoke with a slight accent for, as I later learned, she was French Canadian.

"I see you found the kitchen, Mr. Holmes," noted the Earl, nodding to Holmes' coffee cup. "Mrs. O'Reilly is a gem and I trust you'll agree, she makes the best coffee you've ever had."

"I've certainly had none better," agreed Holmes.

"Ward tells us you are on a case for the American writer, Mark Twain. That must be exciting!" exclaimed the Earl's wife.

"I have found, Countess," replied Holmes, "that the nature and complexity of the crime are more a determinant of the level of 'excitement', as you put it, than the personage of the victim. If you've read Watson's early stories then you will remember that we were in far graver danger when our client was a governess, than when it was a king."

"Ah, you refer to *The Sign of the Four* and *A Scandal in Bohemia*," chimed in the Earl. "I see your point, Mr. Holmes. So this case for Twain may not engender any excitement, or very little then."

"So far it has been an exercise of the mind," responded the sleuth. "The complexity has proved stimulating, but excitement may yet be forthcoming."

(Holmes confided to me later that he did not wish to mention the shooting incident on the train to Ward James' mother, as he felt it was not his place to cause her undue concern.)

At that moment Rupert arrived at the study door to announce that 'breakfast was served'. The trio adjourned to the dining room where the younger James was already standing by. It was he who held the chair for his mother, as his father sat stiffly and hung his cane on the back of his chair.

Breakfast passed with pleasant conversation and afterward Holmes repaired to his room to retrieve his umbrella.

Venturing out once again, he found Johnny in the stable with a closed-in coach, ready for journey.

Holmes hoisted himself inside and requested Johnny to take him to the telegraph office. Making conversation with the young Irishman he asked, "Has Master Ward decided what type of automobile he is going to acquire ?"

"I don't believe so, Mr. Holmes. He's most anxious for the 1000 mile trial coming in April, so he can see all the different types available."

"A wise choice," answered Holmes. "What with his many trips to London, I would imagine he'd want something both fast and reliable."

"Well, it won't be as fast as the Express train," responded Johnny. "But, then again, he'll be able to keep to his own schedule and come and go as he pleases."

"A distinct advantage in his line of work," replied Holmes.

The groom softened his voice, "I wouldn't know about that, sir. He just seems to spend a lot o' time travellin' back and forth on the Earl's business."

"Of course," answered my friend. Changing the subject, he continued, "After I dash off this telegram I shall likely spend the day at the manor. However, I would be obliged if someone can take me into town about four o'clock. I'll be spending the afternoon and evening out and about the Hippodrome and may be quite late, as I expect Watson on the late train."

"I'll be happy to see to it myself, Mr. Holmes. It'll be a pleasure to meet Dr. Watson and do anything I can to help your case."

"Ha! There's a stout fellow! I shall welcome your company."

Chapter Twenty-Two

Now that I have accounted for Holmes' actions while I was in Reading, I feel I can return to the events of that Tuesday afternoon from my own perspective.

Robert sped along quite rapidly after leaving Newbury and it was little more than an hour before we passed through Marlborough. Once we were beyond the western limits of the town, he decided to pull over to the side of the road so that we could stretch our legs.

It was quite necessary to do so, for the combination of speed, turns and bumps in the road had taken their toll on our muscles to maintain our balance in our seats. Unlike the smooth ride of a train on its rails, this mode of transportation called for quite a bit of stamina and exercise. I had just finished smoking a cigarette when Robert asked if I was ready to go again. I had replied in the affirmative when he surprised me with another question.

"Would you like to take a turn at driving, Doctor?"

Now of course I had driven various carts and wagons throughout my life and had even taken the helm of a small boat once. But this offer filled me with both apprehension and excitement.

"I'm afraid I wouldn't know what to do," I responded. "Is this something you can teach me easily?"

"There's nothing to it, Doctor," he answered. "The hardest part is starting and stopping. You control your speed with the throttle here, use the clutch and this lever to change gears as you speed up or slow down and then it's just a matter of watching the road and steering around anything that's in the way."

Recalling my earlier enthusiasm when speaking with the other doctors from the Knightly Lodgings, I readily agreed that this was a skill I was going to have to learn if I were to keep up with the times. Consenting to his tutelage, I climbed up into the driver's seat and did as he instructed, while he started the engine.

Once the chugging of the pistons began, he scampered up into the back seat and leaned forward over my shoulder to give me instructions. It was not quite as easy as he made it sound. I stalled the engine four times while trying to get the gears to engage. Finally, on the fifth try, I had determined the proper pressure needed to release the clutch and engage the throttle smoothly. This, to me, seemed the most difficult of the tasks involved in the operations of the automobile. Of course, I may have been at a disadvantage, with my old war wound and the cold weather conspiring to keep my leg from being as supple as I might have wished.

Once we were moving, I confess that I was euphoric with the speed which I was able to maintain. Steering proved quite easy and, using Robert's goggles to protect my eyes from the dust and grit, I proved quite capable at avoiding holes and rocks and keeping to the road. Shifting gears on the move seemed much easier and the countryside sped by with ease.

After roughly an hour and a half, we approached the town of Chippenham. As we approached, I suddenly found myself rushing toward an intersection where I would be forced to make a decision as to which road to take. Slowing down too rapidly, the engine stalled before I could engage a lower gear. So I pulled over to the side as I let in the clutch and coasted to a stop.

So ended my first experience at operating a motorcar. We stretched our legs again and Robert took over the driving, knowing which roads would keep us on course and far more comfortable at higher speeds. I had kept between twelve and fifteen miles per hour according to the gauge on the dashboard. Robert never dropped below fifteen on the open road. He managed to hit twenty-two on the downhill stretch of Two Mile Hill Road as we descended toward the sea level where Bristol lay.

True to his word, my chauffeur had delivered me into the Bristol city limits by six o'clock. Now that we were in the city, of course, we were required to reduce our speed considerably. Upon asking for directions to the Hippodrome, I found myself deposited at the entrance at six-twenty.

"Are you sure you want me to just leave you here, Doctor?" asked my new young friend. "I'd be happy to take you to a hotel, or on to meet Mr. Holmes."

Retrieving my suitcase and medical bag I replied, "It's quite all right, Robert. Holmes will be along soon, if he's not inside already. Should there be any problem I see that there is a hotel just down there, across the street, where I can find accommodation for the night if need be."

Convinced that my situation was agreeable, he bid me farewell. "All right then, Doctor, if you say so. I hope we meet again."

I reached out to shake his hand, "It's been a pleasure, lad. Thank your mother again for her hospitality, and thank you for letting me have a turn at the tiller of this marvellous machine."

"You're quite welcome, Doctor. Goodbye and good luck with your case."

He chugged off down the street, keeping to a very slow speed now that it was beyond sunset. His vehicle had no running lights and he was dependent upon the illumination of the street lamps.

We had come south, down St. Augustine's Parade to reach this destination. Further along, however, a sign indicated that the street continued as Anchor Road. The hotel, I now saw, graced a separate, parallel thoroughfare on the far side of a broad patch of green.

I turned toward the theatre. The Hippodrome[1] is certainly not as imposing an edifice as the Lyceum in London, with its magnificent columns and Greek architecture. Externally, at any rate, it was as plain as any of the shops in the street, but above the entrance large white letters on a red background

---

[1] Watson's memory appears to have failed him at this point. The Hippodrome in Bristol was not built until 1912. It is more likely that he meant the Threate Royal on King Street, which is in the same neighbourhood.

proclaimed the name 'Hippodrome'. The box office, to the left as I faced it, was likewise painted red on the ground floor, with large windows.

I entered and must have appeared an odd sight, carrying my suitcase and medical bag with me. There were only two couples in line for tickets. The show was not scheduled until seven o'clock. I patiently waited my turn and soon was identifying myself to the assistant.

"Ah, yes, Dr. Watson, we have been expecting you. Please go around to that door and we will take you to see your patient."

'**Patient?**' I wondered, but chose to remain silent as I did not know what Holmes might have implied to these people in an effort to get close to this Smith fellow.

I strode through the door indicated and was greeted by an usher. He relieved me of my luggage and put it aside for safekeeping. He bade me follow and I was escorted to an office up on the second floor. He opened the door for me and I found Holmes seated on a sofa opposite a large walnut desk with brass fittings. The man behind the desk had a folder in front of him, and more stacked in piles to his left. Off to one side of the room were large windows with four comfortable upholstered chairs facing them. From what I could gather, these windows lay just beneath the upper balcony and afforded a magnificent view of the stage. When a performance was in progress they could be open to allow voices and sound effects to be heard.

Holmes stood upon my entrance and introduced me.

"Watson, your timing is impeccable. Allow me to introduce Mr. Ruben Walker, the theatre manager. Mr. Walker, my friend and colleague, Dr. John Watson."

Mr. Walker rose and shook my hand. He was a well-built man, some five foot six inches tall and roughly forty years of age. His grip was firm. His black hair was shot throughout with streaks of grey, as were his moustache and goatee. His brown eyes were distorted by a gold-rimmed pince-nez, its black ribbon trailing down to a button upon his lapel.

"Welcome, Doctor," he replied. "Please, sit down. Would you care for some refreshment? Brandy, sherry, perhaps?"

"A small sherry would be welcome, Mr. Walker. I'm afraid I've a bit of a chill from my journey."

"Ah yes, Holmes told me you were coming from Reading by motor car. That must have been quite a ride."

"I imagine my muscles will be paying for it tomorrow," I replied, taking the warming sherry as I sat, "But it did allow me to arrive here three hours ahead of the train.

"Now then," I continued, turning to Sherlock Holmes, "what's this about a patient?"

"A little ruse, dear fellow," he smiled, as he lit a cigarette, "Officially, I am here as William Scott, an agent of Sir Henry Irving, seeking out new talent. However, I have a medical condition that requires the attendance of my personal physician from time to time."

"I see," I replied. "Thus giving us both access to the theatre and the actors without tipping off Smith as to our actual reason for being here."

"Precisely. Only Mr. Walker knows our true purpose."

"A purpose I believe to be a waste of time," responded the manager. "Arthur is no thief. He is a very talented actor with excellent prospects that would make it unnecessary to steal another performer's material."

"From what I have gathered thus far," replied Holmes, "that seems to be the general consensus. None of his fellow actors, nor even the stage hands, reveal even a hint of suspicion against the man. One or two have exhibited signs of jealousy at his skill, but the overall impression being imparted to me, as Irving's agent, is that Irving's troupe would be lucky to have him."

"Have you spoken to the man himself?" I asked.

"I have elected to wait until after his performance for that confrontation," answered my friend. "Much can be discerned about a man's character through his ability as an actor."

"I would think all good criminals would be good actors to some extent," interjected Walker. "After all, they must be able to act naturally in stressful situations and keep cool under pressure."

"Yes," Holmes responded, "but there are signals that can give even accomplished actors away. With the front balcony seats you have arranged for us, I should be able to determine our friend's methods and style before we meet him afterwards. That will give me an advantage that he may not be prepared for."

"Humpf! I still say you've got the wrong man."

"A distinct possibility, but let us not leave any stone unturned."

"Well," replied the manager, "the show starts in twenty minutes. Would you like to start down to your seats?"

Walker led us down a stairwell and around to an entrance to the grand circle, just above stage right. "Tuesday crowds are always lighter than most," he explained. "So your timing is fortunate to be able to use these seats." He opened the door for us, "Enjoy the show. Shall I see you afterwards?"

"We shall either stop by or leave a message for you," answered Holmes, "Thank you again for your assistance."

We took our seats and I must admit it was a comfort after so many hours of bouncing along in Robert's Daimler.

An usher provided us with programmes. I perused the cast, looking for Smith's name. Holmes seeing that I could not find it pointed out, "His given name is Arthur, Watson. He's playing the part of Gregorio."

After a few minutes, the lights dimmed and the play commenced. It wasn't long before 'Gregorio' made his entrance. He had come from stage right. At first, his back was to us. Soon, however, his character turned to face the audience.

What I saw at that moment was something I shall not soon forget. I leaned forward in my seat, trying to adjust my eyes to what I could not believe they were seeing.

I felt a tap at my arm and there Holmes was, holding out a pair of opera glasses which he had taken the foresight to bring.

I took them with a whispered 'thank you' and focused on the young man's face. I discovered later that he was less than two weeks shy of his twenty-fifth birthday. What I saw through the lenses of the opera glasses confirmed my initial impression and stirred up my memories of my first meeting with Sherlock Holmes. For on that stage, I beheld an exact image of the man to whom Stamford had introduced me back in 1881.

Chapter Twenty-Three

I looked over at Holmes, mouth agape. He said quietly, "Uncanny, is it not?"

"Unbelievable," I whispered. "Were you not sitting here I should swear that somehow I had travelled twenty years backward aboard H. G. Wells' time machine.[1]"

"The resemblance is rather remarkable," he responded.

At a look of annoyance from others seated in the grand circle who objected to our conversing, we ceased our discussion and took in the rest of the play in relative silence. As we did so I took the time to appreciate the interior of the theatre. Its classic styling, ornate ceiling and richly carved ornamentation belied its modest exterior. It was every bit as luxurious, if not quite as large, as most theatres I'd attended in London. I am convinced that whoever the manufacturers of theatre seats are, they only carry red velvet upholstery, for it seems every theatre is thus furnished. Therefore red becomes a predominant colour of the rest of the décor.

Afterwards, we made our way backstage and found the young man in his dressing room.

Another actor, with whom he shared this accommodation, was leaving just as we arrived. Thus we had him all to ourselves. Holmes closed the door and addressed him.

"A.W. Smith, I presume," said the detective.

Smith, who had been seated in front of his dressing mirror stood and offered his hand.

"You must be Mr. Scott?" he enquired. "I've heard you were asking about me."

Holmes cleared his throat and replied, "Ahem, I am afraid I have created a false impression which I must now

---

[1] H.G. Wells novel, *The Time Machine* was published in 1895

correct. My name is Sherlock Holmes and this is my colleague, Dr. John Watson. While I am indeed a close acquaintance of Sir Henry Irving, I am not actually here on his behalf. We are investigating a crime that took place while you were staying at the Langham Hotel in London."

I watched his face for any sign of guilty reaction, but he revealed nothing, except possibly confusion. Instead, he waved us to sit down and returned to his own chair.

"I see," he replied, obviously disappointed that we were not there to give a boost to his career. "What is it that you need from me?"

Holmes spoke up, "A theft took place in the room directly below yours, sometime during the night of Thursday last. There is some evidence that the fire escape, which your rooms shared, may have been used."

"Really?" he responded. "I didn't hear anything about any theft. What was stolen?"

"Some papers that may have value to certain persons," Holmes replied. "Did you notice anything outside your window that evening, say between six and midnight?"

He sat back thoughtfully, "Thursday night, you say? Was that the night it rained?"

"Yes, and there may have been some thunder as well."

"Oh, yes. It seems to me I did hear some thunder in the distance, just before I left for dinner."

"Do you recall what time that was?" asked Holmes, leaning forward to study the man's face as he answered.

"I left for dinner at about seven-fifteen, so some time before that I would imagine."

"Where did you dine and how long were you gone?" pressed the detective.

Smith reflexively replied, "I met a friend at Simpson's and was back around ten o'clock." Then he narrowed his gaze at my friend and asked, "Why?"

Holmes leaned back in his chair and answered candidly, "To be quite frank, sir, the papers in question would be of particular value to someone in your profession."

Smith's hand went to his chest, fingers splayed out as he exclaimed, "You think *I* was the thief? Are you serious?"

"Calm yourself, sir," I interposed. "We are speaking to everyone whose room was in the vicinity. No one has accused you."

"No?" he replied, standing and waving his hand in his agitation. "You follow me all the way from London, you lie about who you are. You speak to everyone about me, invading my privacy. You may well have caused damage to my career. Now people who thought you represented Irving will think I wasn't good enough when you fail to offer me a situation with his troupe. Even if you do not accuse me, your presence is an insult and unworthy of gentlemen!"

"My methods may seem unorthodox to you, Mr. Smith," replied Holmes calmly, as he also stood. "But through them, I am now convinced you had nothing to do with this theft. We shall not trouble you any further. Come, Watson, we have taken up enough of Mr. Smith's time."

I stood to join my friend, but directed one last query at the actor.

"Just one further point, Mr. Smith: why do you use the name 'Arthur Wontner' as your stage name?"

He deigned to satisfy my curiosity and replied, "'Wontner' is my middle name, Doctor. It helps me retain my identity without becoming lost among the masses who share the common surname of 'Smith'."

"Thank you, sir. Good luck with your career. If tonight's performance was any indication of your talent, I am sure you will be a success."

"Thank you," he replied, only slightly mollified, and his 'Good night' was spat out as brusquely as any I've ever heard.[1]

*****

---

[1] Arthur Wontner would go on to a fine acting career and would become best known for playing Sherlock Holmes in five films from 1931 to 1937. His eldest son, Hugh Wontner, would become Lord Mayor of London in 1973.

Following Holmes out into the hall I asked, as we walked, "How is it that you are sure he is not the thief, Holmes?"

"It is a matter of the study of human reactions, Watson. Someday I must write a monograph on the subject. However, in observing the young man closely, the way he positioned his body, his hands, his feet, all were quite telling. As were his facial expressions, for even the slightest reactions of the mouth and the eyes can speak volumes. No, he is not our thief, Doctor."

"Are you sure you are not reading yourself into that somewhat, old fellow?" I asked. "After all, his resemblance to you might have affected your judgment."

He stopped and looked at me quite indignantly, "Really, Watson? Deductive reasoning is a science primarily: while there is some art involved, it does not lend itself to avoidance of facts. Smith's physiognomy would certainly include the same muscle combinations as my own where the resemblance is strong, thus making those reactions appear similar. However, his life experiences, and influences of parents, relatives, friends, or even persons with whom he trained toward his profession, would add to those reactions. While there are certain movements common to nearly all persons under stress, or when they attempt to deceive, it is a capital mistake to assume that everyone reveals himself in the same way. This is why one must study the individual for a time, to learn his particular mannerisms, before drawing conclusions."

"And have any of our suspects exhibited suspicious mannerisms?" I enquired.

"There have been a few tell-tale signs from more than one," he replied as he turned to continue our exit. "However, I have not yet been able to line up the facts and timelines with enough assurance to draw a definite conclusion."

We stopped by Walker's office to offer our farewells. He, being naturally curious, asked the obvious.

"Well, Mr. Holmes, are you convinced now that Arthur is not your man?"

"I am, Mr. Walker, and I quite agree with you, that he holds much promise as an actor."

"Ha!" he exclaimed. "I told you so. It's too bad you're not really here to represent Sir Henry Irving. The lad deserves a chance like that."

Holmes nodded and replied, "My ruse served my purpose. However, I do count Sir Henry among my friends and I promise you that I shall recommend that he keep any eye on young Arthur Wontner for the future."

"He'll be happy to hear that," answered the theatre manager.

"I prefer that you do not mention it," countered the detective. "Nothing is guaranteed and I should rather keep my name out of it."

"As you wish, Mr. Holmes," Walker extended his hand in farewell and we both shook it and bid him adieu.

Retrieving my luggage, we ventured out into the chill night. In front of the theatre a light mist had turned the wide street into a series of shining spotlights, where the reflections of the street lamps erupted from the wet pavement, illuminating the misty drops like fireflies, as the fog rolled in from the Bristol Channel.

"Where to now, Holmes?" I asked.

"Yon tavern holds our transport, Watson," he replied, pointing his umbrella up the street. "Lord Roseboro's driver awaits us there. We shall rouse him from his evening's libations to return us to the Roseboro estate for the night."

Chapter Twenty-Four

O'Reilly skilfully navigated the wet roads back to Roseboro and we found ourselves shaking off our wet coats in the entrance hall, precisely as the clock in the study could just be discerned striking midnight.

Rupert met us and took our coats. He announced that there was coffee being kept warm in the kitchen, then informed me my room would be next to Holmes' as he departed to deposit my luggage there.

Sitting down on a kitchen stool beside the stove, I gratefully took the steaming coffee cup that Holmes had poured for me.

Its warmth, as it slid down my throat, was a welcome balm to the chills I had experienced on the drive from Reading and the damp of the evening itself.

As my chest responded to its recuperative powers, I suddenly noticed its wonderful aftertaste on my tongue and the vapours that seemed to massage my sinuses.

I looked up at my companion who was standing beside me with his back to the stove, enjoying its warmth.

"Good lord, Holmes, what is this ?" I exclaimed.

Holmes finished a sip himself and glanced down at me.

"This, Doctor, is Mrs. O'Reilly's famous Irish coffee, or at least famous within this house. It is a particular favourite of Lord Roseboro."

"I can imagine," I replied, downing another swallow. "This must be at least one third whisky!"

"It is rather stronger than my earlier serving," Holmes conceded. "Perhaps the gracious cook has taken into account the chill of the evening."

We drained our cups and Holmes poured a second round, which we sipped rather more slowly. At last, we decided, it was time for bed.

Holmes informed me that the household breakfasted at eight o'clock and bid me goodnight as he left me at the room that Rupert's staff had prepared. A well-built fire was blazing in the hearth and the room was most comfortable. The exertions of the day, no doubt assisted by Mrs. O'Reilly's elixir, sent me into a deep sleep the moment my head fell into the soft down pillow.

The next morning I awoke to the sound of the fire being built up by one of the menservants. As quiet as he was attempting to be, the sounds of the logs being piled and occasionally slipping, was still making its way through my fog-shrouded brain.

I propped myself up on one elbow and asked, "What time is it?"

"Beggin' your pardon, Doctor," the young fellow replied, "I did not mean to wake you, sir."

"It's quite all right," I responded. Then I noticed a bright glow at the bottom of the room-darkening drapes on the window and repeated my earlier query.

"It's nearly ten, Doctor. Mr. Holmes asked us not to disturb you, after your long ordeal of yesterday. Cook will fix you up some breakfast whenever you are ready."

"Ten o'clock?" I questioned. Then I rubbed my eyes with my free hand and felt a buzzing sensation in my nose that quickly led to a sneeze.

"God bless you, sir," piped up the lad automatically. "Would you like another blanket, sir?"

I sneezed again, then took stock of my body. As I expected, the muscles of my back and legs were protesting against the previous day's abuse. My primary concern, however, was an overall clamminess to my skin which felt as if I had been subjected to a bout of night sweats.

"No, thank you …"I answered, hesitating, trying to remember if the boy had given his name.

Sensing my predicament he replied, "Bobby, sir".

"No thank you, Bobby. Frankly I'm not feeling very well. Would it be possible to get some hot tea?"

"I'll run right down for it, Doctor Watson. Cream, or sugar?"

"A spoonful of sugar would be sufficient, thank you. Oh, where is the W.C.?" I asked, as I pushed myself into a sitting position.

"Out the door to your left and second door on the left, it's just beyond Mr. Holmes' room. I'll be back in a trice with your tea, sir."

"Thank you, Bobby," I called as he left. I managed to stand, though feeling somewhat light-headed. Fortunately my cane was next to the bed stand. Donning my dressing gown, I made my way to perform my morning ablutions.

Once there, I realized that I had been there the night before and felt rather foolish for having forgotten. I made my stay as quick as possible, however, for though I am sure the house was quite comfortable, I began to shiver as I returned to my room. I quickly dived back under the covers for warmth, but was still shaking when Bobby returned.

On his heels, as he entered with my tea, was Holmes, accompanied by Lady Roseboro herself.

"Forgive me, Doctor," she said, "but I cannot sit by while a guest of mine is ill. Let me check your temperature."

I started to tell her where my thermometer was in my medical bag, but the back of her hand was already against my forehead. She persisted in checking my cheeks and the back of my neck, clucking like a mother French hen, for her accent was stronger when her speech was less formal.

"You have a fever, but it is not too strong," she stated. "You must rest and drink much fluids. I will have Cook make you some chicken broth. Have you any Aspirin[1] in your bag?"

I nodded in the affirmative and she fetched a dose, mixed it with water and insisted I drink it down.

She then bade Bobby to fetch a servant's bell, which I could ring if I needed anything. Her French pronunciation accented the vowels in his name, which made it come out "Bow-bay".

---

[1] Chemically known as acetylsalicylic acid, discovered in 1853. A new, easier digesting formula was named Aspirin by the German company Bayer AG and by1899 was selling around the world.

Somehow, in my feverish stupor, that appeared quite amusing. Holmes, meanwhile, stood back waiting to get a word in.

Finally she made her exit, insisting that I ring for any need. Then she addressed Holmes.

"Your friend needs rest, Mr. Holmes. We must let him sleep so that his fever can break."

Holmes gave a slight bow in deference to both her rank and her position as our hostess.

"I shall be but a moment, Lady Roseboro. I must confer briefly with the Doctor."

"Quickly, if you please, Mr. Holmes," she commanded and left us alone.

"She is quite formidable, Holmes," I observed.

"Yes, Watson, she brings the practicality of her background as a nurse in Quebec into her station as a Countess in Bristol."

"She was a nurse?" I queried. "However did she come to marry Lord Roseboro?"

"As I understand it, they met when he was still just Harrison James, the heir to Roseboro. He was on a business trip in Canada when he fell ill and she nursed him back to health."

"In ... inter ... achoo!"

"Enough for now, Watson. I shall be off this morning to send some telegrams, but I shall return by noon should you need anything."

"What of the investigation, Holmes?" I asked. "Surely you need to return to London."

"I can follow many of my trails via the telegraph for now, and a day or two here in Bristol may actually prove quite fruitful."

My head was feeling stuffy and thus my brain refused to follow his train of thought, so I lay back on the pillow and surrendered to Morpheus with a "Whatever you say, Holmes."

Chapter Twenty-Five

The next time I awoke it was well into the afternoon. I was considering another trip down the hall when Bobby poked his head in.

"Ah, you're awake, Doctor. Her Ladyship wishes to know if you feel up to eating something?"

I considered his question for a moment and realized I was starving.

"Yes, Bobby, some of that broth she mentioned might just hit the spot. Perhaps some biscuits or bread as well?"

"I'll see to it straight away, sir. Do you need any help?"

I had swivelled my legs around to sit on the side of the bed.

"I think I can manage, if you'll just hand me my dressing gown."

He did as I asked and stood by me as I slipped it on. I put a hand on his shoulder as I reached for my cane and then freed him for his duties.

"Thank you, Bobby, I shall be alright now."

He retreated out the door and down the stairs two at a time, as I retraced my steps from earlier that morning. On my return trip to my room I nearly collided with Holmes as he strode around the corner, busily engaged in reading a telegram.

"Watson!" he exclaimed. "Good to see you about! Feeling any better, old fellow?"

"The fever seems lower, if not gone, but I am feeling somewhat weak and lightheaded."

"Have you eaten anything?"

"I've just dispatched the boy for some broth. Hopefully it will sit well. What have you been up to?"

"Ah, I am in correspondence with Hopkins on certain matters and have dispatched further instructions to

Shinwell Johnson. We shall see how those answers turn our case, for I believe I am closing in."

By now I was crawling back in to bed and, though tired, I was alert with curiosity. I sat up with the pillows supporting my back, prepared for a bed tray whenever Bobby returned, and asked Holmes for more details.

"What have you got Johnson looking into? John Clay's business?"

"Among others," he replied, enigmatically. "I am attempting to eliminate motives among those possible perpetrators of Clemens' papers. While Johnson scrutinizes the underworld, Hopkins is researching the supposedly above-board suspects, along certain avenues which I have laid out for him."

"Then you should be getting back to London, Holmes. You mustn't allow my indisposition to jeopardize your case."

"Quite the contrary, dear fellow," he replied. "The case is progressing quite nicely with me here. I can certainly spare a day or two before returning. You must rest and regain your strength. I dare not return you to the widow Savage in such a deplorable condition."

The thought of Adelaide brought a smile to my face and that moment was when Lady Roseboro entered, followed by Bobby with a bed tray containing steaming chicken broth and fresh baked rolls.

She came to the side of my bed and felt my forehead again with the back of her hand.

"Ah, you are much improved, Dr. Watson. It appears your fever has broken. You must eat and regain your strength, but not too fast. Your stomach acids are busy fighting the mucus drained from your sinuses. They will not stand long against another invasion from having too much food to absorb too quickly and you certainly do not wish them to go into retreat."

I must admit that her quaint, French-accented, description of a process I knew so well by its scientific explanation was charming. I could not help but smile as I thanked her and Bobby as he set the tray across my lap.

"Here is another dose of Aspirin, Doctor," she ordered as she set the packet down next to a glass of water. "Wait until you've eaten at least half your broth before you take it."

"Yes, Lady Roseboro, thank you for your kindness," I replied.

"*Ce n'est rien.* It is nothing, Dr. Watson," she replied, "merely the duties of a good hostess."

She turned to Holmes.

"Your friend is much better, Mr. Holmes," she observed to my companion. "But he should stay in bed and rest after he eats."

Holmes could not help but notice the underlying command in her voice and the look in her eye.

"I promise you, Lady Roseboro, I shall not overstay his meal."

She nodded and left, with Bobby at her heels.

Eating slowly was an easy feat, for the broth was almost scalding hot. The rolls, on the other hand, were deliciously warm and soft. Mrs. O'Reilly had somehow achieved a buttery taste that needed no external spread or additional flavor to compete with its natural goodness.

"Holmes, these are delicious. Here, you must try one," I said, lifting the plate toward him.

He held up his hand, "Save them for your own recuperation, dear fellow. I have had my fill at breakfast this morning."

I set the plate back down to one side and attempted the broth again. The steam rising from the bowl invaded my sinuses and made my eyes water. After sufficiently blowing on the spoonful I'd extracted, I was able, at last, to down a swallow. Its heat and saltiness assaulted my throat, which I had not realized had become so sore or swollen, but its taste was a godsend and I continued to slowly down several spoonfuls as Holmes filled me in on the goings on of the day.

"The younger James was quite correct in his assertion that Roseboro is a very active household," he related. "Having last night's storm pass by has left a sunny day for visitors to pop in and out. One being of particular interest to us."

"Really?" I asked, setting aside my spoon.

He motioned for me to keep eating and continued, "As I returned from my morning journey to the telegraph office, I came into the foyer to find Mr. Reese handing a packet to Ward James. It was a typical lawyer's envelope, tied with string and sealed with wax."

"What significance do you attach to this, Holmes? Reese is the family solicitor. Wouldn't it be natural for him to deliver sealed documents in person?"

"Quite so, Watson," he responded. "However, the sealing wax was green."

"Green?" I replied. "That is a bit unusual, I suppose, since red is the most popular colour, but what does it matter?"

"The British Crown has a colour coded system for sealing documents, Doctor. Green is one of its levels of secrecy," he answered.

"Is it a government document?" I asked, sipping the last spoonful of my broth.

"I have not been able to ascertain that. James was quite able to act naturally upon my entrance and nonchalantly turned the document away before I could note the seal's impression. Reese, on the other hand, was rather nonplussed by my appearance. It was at this point, however, that Lord Roseboro intervened and called them both into the study."

I set the bed tray to one side, poured my Aspirin into my water glass and downed a generous gulp. Turning back to Holmes I asked, "Do you think it relates to our case, Holmes?"

He sighed and patted my shoulder, "I do not know, my friend. For now it is an anomaly that I shall keep tucked away for the future if it appears significant. Now, you get some rest. I shall look in on you later."

He took the tray himself, rather than ring for the boy and lightly shoved the door closed with his foot as he departed.

I settled back into the pillows, not holding out much hope of sleeping since I had already been in bed for well over twelve hours. Thoughts of our case drifted about my brain. I attempted to sort through them, looking for a link, or a singular incident or remark that might lead to a solution. As I contemplated Holmes' observation of the green sealing wax, Lewis Carroll's words came to mind,

> "The time has come," the Walrus said,
> "To talk of many things:
> Of shoes – and ships – and sealing-wax –
> Of cabbages – and kings – ..."[1]

---

[1] *Through the Looking Glass* published in 1871.

Chapter Twenty-Six

The next thing I knew, Bobby was rebuilding the fire and sunlight no longer filtered under the drapes. As my eyes adjusted to the darkness of the room, lit only by the orange and yellow glow of the fire, I found myself once again asking Bobby for the time.

"It's a quarter to six, Doctor. Can I get you anything?"

I took stock of myself and was disconcerted to discover a grumbling in my intestines. Sitting up too quickly as I swung my legs over the side of the bed, a wave of dizziness assaulted me and I nearly fell.

"If you could, help me to the toilet, and be quick about it!" I rasped.

Forgoing my dressing gown and leaning on the lad for support, I managed to make it just in time. When I came out again, Bobby was waiting with my dressing gown and slippers. I bundled up against the chill as I retreated back to my room.

The fire was blazing and the blankets were warm as toast. The dizziness left once I found myself horizontal again. A few minutes later, Bobby returned with Lady Roseboro.

Checking my pulse and temperature, she pronounced me normal and on the road to recovery.

"Your illness has left you, Dr. Watson, in the usual fashion," she stated with a nurse's efficiency.

"I am sorry to be such a bother, Lady Roseboro," I apologized.

"Marriage may have made me a Countess, Doctor, but I am still a nurse by training and I'll not allow illness in my household. Do you feel up to eating?"

I answered in the affirmative and within a quarter hour a bed tray containing vegetable soup, crackers and rolls was deposited in my lap.

Holmes also joined me for dinner, with a tray of his own set upon a small table that was moved over by the bed so that we could converse.

"So, Watson, how are you feeling?" he asked.

"A little weak, but on the mend, Holmes," I replied. "I should think we could return to London tomorrow, or Friday at the latest."

"Splendid, old friend, you rested well this afternoon then?"

"Surprisingly yes, but I had the most extraordinary dream."

"Really, pray tell?"

"It must have been your mention of the green sealing wax. Lewis Carroll's poem came to mind as I was drifting off. In my dream there was a walrus, wearing a mourning coat and top hat, with a broad red sash running across his torso diagonally. He tore off a bright green cabbage leaf and melted it like a candle to let the wax drip on the lock of Clemens' briefcase. Then a seal came along, wearing a crown, and punched an impression upon it with its nose."

"Ha!" he cried in laughter. "Your imagination is quite intact, Doctor, and your mind is working in mysterious ways."

"Still, a dreamless sleep would be preferable, Holmes. Perhaps tonight I shall take a sleeping draught and see what the morrow brings."

"An excellent idea," he replied and then asked, "Would you care for some wine, Watson? It is quite excellent."

"A small glass perhaps," I countered.

"What of Reese?" I remembered, as I swallowed the sweet, white Bordeaux. "Did you learn any more along that line?"

"He returned to London on the afternoon express. I did spend some time alone in the study later, but the remnants of the envelope were destroyed in the fireplace and the wax melted to the point where the impression was beyond recognition."

"Pity, well I doubt it had anything to do with our case at any rate. More likely some business venture of the Earl's," I stated.

"Yes, very likely," replied Holmes, rather distractedly. He then stood and raised his glass, "To your health, Doctor. Sleep well. I shall be spending considerable time at the telegraph office in the morning. I shall likely not see you until noon or so. Good night."

"Good night, Holmes," I replied, rather taken aback by this sudden departure. However, I have learned over the years that the mind of Holmes also works in mysterious ways.

*****

The next morning I was feeling much better and managed to dress and make it downstairs for breakfast with the family. Lord Roseboro greeted me heartily from the head of the table where he had already seated himself. Ward James was just pushing in his mother's chair and pulled out the one next to her for me. I gratefully sat down and he went 'round to his father's left and sat as well.

"I must apologize, Dr. Watson," said his Lordship. "I should have been up to see you, but Jenny insisted that you may have been contagious and I just recently recovered from a bout of influenza. I trust you are feeling well again?"

"I believe I am over the worst part," I replied. "Just a matter of regaining strength now, thanks to your wife's ministrations."

"More likely Mrs. O'Reilly's cooking," responded the Countess. "But I am glad you are feeling better, Doctor."

Rupert enquired if we were ready and the Earl advised him to go ahead and have breakfast served, as Holmes would not be joining us.

Young Ward asked, "How are your investigations coming along, Doctor? I know Mr. Holmes has been wearing out the telegraph lines between here and London."

"As usual in such matters," I answered, "Holmes has not confided all to me. He prefers to have his proofs well in hand when he gets close to the end of a case. Then his penchant for the dramatic takes over and all is revealed in one final dissertation."

"Really?" questioned Roseboro, "He has it solved then?"

"He must feel he is getting close, your Lordship, for he is in that stage that alternates between a flurry of activity and single-minded concentration that occupies his mind and body to the exclusion of food, rest and lengthy conversation."

"Any ideas yourself, Doctor?" enquired the son.

"Personally, I've always leaned toward the former convict who was in the room below Clemens. But that may just be my own prejudices from our past dealings with him."

"Yes, I've heard of the claims of the alleged Duke of Dartford." he replied. "I should not be surprised if your leanings are correct, Doctor."

The food arrived and we settled in to a hearty meal. I dared not stuff myself, though the temptation was powerful. I contented myself with eggs and toast with a mild tea to wash it down.

Afterwards, the Earl offered me his study with its vast quantity of books. Through the windows, I could see that it had rained during the night and the cloud covering was still dark and gloomy. Fortunately, the room was well lit and a substantial fire kept it quite comfortable.

I was tempted to pick up Lewis Carroll, but chose to indulge myself with Edgar Allan Poe instead. I was enjoying Poe's detective works and had just finished the story of Dupin and *The Purloined Letter* when Holmes entered, striding immediately to the fire to warm himself from his trip to the telegraph office.

"You are looking much better today, Watson," he exclaimed. "How are you feeling?"

"I am nearly myself again, Holmes. Perhaps a little weak, but my symptoms have succumbed to Lady Roseboro's ministrations and Mrs. O'Reilly's cooking."

"Excellent! Do you feel up to taking the train back to London this afternoon?"

"That is an express, is it not?" I enquired.

He smiled, "Yes, old friend, it will have us back in London in less than three hours."

"Then I shall be ready," I stated with as much bravado as I could muster. "When do we leave?"

"I'll arrange for Johnny to take us to the station. The train leaves at four, so we should be off by three o'clock in order to be able to purchase our tickets."

"Plenty of time then," I noted, as it was only eleven-fifteen. "In fact I think I shall go up and pack now, then catch another nap to bolster my strength."

"An excellent plan, Doctor. If you are not awake I shall arouse you by two-thirty."

I returned Poe to the shelf and decided to take the study's spiral staircase to the upper floor where my bedroom awaited.

Holmes, I noted, strode over to see what I had been reading. He gazed up at me with a 'Hmpf!' as I made my exit.

Chapter Twenty-Seven

I managed to sleep soundly and awoke just after two o'clock. I completed my packing and laid out my overcoat and bowler. I strode over to Holmes' room and found it empty, save for his own luggage by the door. Perhaps I should amend that statement. It was empty of persons, but the room itself was quite filled with the remnants of smoke from Holmes' pipe. The bluish haze would certainly have to be aired out before the next occupant. I could not begin to guess at how many pipes Holmes had smoked during the course of his stay.

I used the facilities and found, to my relief, that everything was back to normal. This eased my mind for the upcoming carriage ride and train trip. Descending the stairs, I noted my host and his son in the study. The Earl was behind his desk and young Ward leaning over to look at some papers.

"Dr. Watson," exclaimed Lord Roseboro, "Come in, sir. Holmes tells us you are both returning to London this afternoon. I am sorry that your visit was so brief. I should have liked to discuss more of the cases you have worked together."

The son excused himself and left with some papers, telling his father that he would take care of the matter in hand.

I took the seat which Roseboro indicated and politely turned down his offer of a cigar.

"I am afraid my throat is a bit sore from my illness," I explained.

"Oh yes, quite right," he responded. "Well, can we look forward to any more of Mr. Holmes adventures being written up any time soon? You have an excellent way with words, Doctor. I am sure the public is anxious for more."

"Holmes has been quite clear on that point," I admitted, reluctantly. "However, lately I have considered that perhaps I could express his cases in a more fictionalized fashion. If I write under a *nom de plume* and change the names of the characters and the dates of the events, it may provide a satisfactory solution for Holmes, myself and the public."

"Well, that would certainly be better than the vacuum we are all experiencing at this point," he stated. "Ah, there's our famous detective now."

Holmes had appeared in the doorway. "Good afternoon, Doctor," he called, "Still feeling up for the trip?"

"Indeed, Holmes, I am all packed," I responded.

"Excellent! May I suggest that you call in at Mrs. O'Reilly's kitchen? You've not eaten lunch and it will be dinner time by the time we arrive at Baker Street."

I weighed this advice and, finding it sound, I excused myself from our host's company to seek out his most obliging cook.

Holmes took my vacated seat and accepted one of his Lordship's fine cigars.

"These are most excellent, Lord Roseboro," he declared, slowly exhaling and enjoying the taste and aroma. "I should introduce you to our client. Mr. Clemens' taste in tobacco leaves much to be desired."

"I find that most Americans' tastes in the finer things fall into that category," the Earl responded.

"*Touche'*," replied the detective. "Clemens is a remarkable man, however, despite his taste, or rather, lack thereof, in cigars. Have you read his works?"

In response to this question the Earl pointed across the room with his cigar and said, "Over there by the fireplace? That whole bookcase is my American author collection. The works of 'Mark Twain' comprise that entire third shelf."

"Yes, I noticed them earlier when Watson returned the selection of Poe which he had been reading. But collecting and reading are not the same thing, your Lordship."

Roseboro smiled around the cigar, now clenched in his teeth, "You are correct, Mr. Holmes. I must admit that my penchant for collecting books has far out distanced my capacity to read them."

He removed the cigar and stubbed it out in the ashtray on his desk, "As far as Mark Twain goes, I have only read *Following the Equator* and *A Connecticut Yankee in King Arthur's Court*. Both of them I found humorous and interesting, to see the world and old England from an American viewpoint."

Holmes nodded, "Clemens does have a unique way of expressing his views through his characters. It would be interesting, indeed, to read his autobiography, should it be recovered."

The Earl lay his hands flat upon the desktop and leaned forward,

"The papers stolen were his autobiography?" he exclaimed in surprise.

"Yes," replied Holmes, extinguishing his own cigar. "Fortunately they are not *all* of his notes. Should we fail in our mission I would imagine that he will be delayed, but not derailed from completing his work."

"But Clemens is rather elderly, is he not?" asked Roseboro, with concern. "Will his health allow for such a delay?"

"If you were to meet him," replied Holmes, "you would find him hale and hearty. He is convinced that he is destined to live until the return of Halley's comet, under which he was born the last time it graced our skies."[1]

"And when is that due to occur?"

"I really have no idea. I rarely keep track of such things unless they are pertinent to my work," the detective replied, off-handedly.

---

[1] Mark Twain is quoted as saying "I came in with Halley's Comet in 1835 ... and I expect to go out with it. It will be the greatest disappointment of my life if I don't go out with Halley's Comet. The Almighty has said, no doubt: 'Now here are these two unaccountable freaks; they came in together, they must go out together.'" Twain died on the 21st April 1910, while Halley's Comet was visible from Earth.

"No matter, I suppose," sighed the Earl. "However, for his sake, and the sake of his readers, I do hope you recover his papers quickly."

"If they have not been destroyed, I believe we have an excellent chance," replied Holmes. "My suspect list is narrowing daily. I have high hopes that when I return to London I will have the answers I need to bring the matter to a close."

"Who would destroy his papers?" asked Roseboro, incredulously.

"There we get back to motive, your Lordship. Obviously, destruction was not the original intent, or they would have been thrown into the fire in Clemens' suite. However, once examined, it is possible that the thief only cared about certain documents, or perhaps what he was looking for wasn't there. If so, he may have destroyed the rest so as not to get caught with them."

"That is unspeakable!" cried the Earl.

"Yes, I imagine to a collector, such as yourself, the destruction of such documents is a sin of great magnitude. However, if the documents have fallen into the hands of such a collector, they may not be seen again for years."

"Unacceptable, Holmes, books are meant to be read and shared, not collecting dust or on display for show! I have admitted that I have not read all the books you see here, but it is my intention to do so, as time and health permits me to."

"Commendable, your Lordship," replied my friend. "However there exists in this world others, who merely wish to possess. A criminal such as that is much harder to capture."

"Well, I certainly wish you success, Mr. Holmes. Ah, here's Dr. Watson. I'll have Johnny bring the carriage round."

*****

The ride to the train station was comfortable, thanks to the enclosed carriage and travelling rugs provided by Lord Roseboro. We were grateful for the warmth, as it had rained during the night and was quite cold outside.

At such short notice Holmes was unable to reserve a private compartment on the London express, but we did manage to find comfortable seats to ourselves in one of the passenger cars.

This time, the journey passed quickly, as I read a newspaper and nodded off a bit, while Holmes mulled over his pipe.

My companion nudged me awake when we pulled into Victoria Station. I was surprised to see that the previous night's storm in Bristol had become much colder as it moved eastward over London and covered the city in snow.

As the sun was setting, barely peeking out between the horizon and the cloud cover like a pale, half-closed, jaundiced eye, the temperature was dropping fast. The snowfall was gaining in intensity. Holmes was fortunate to flag down a growler so that we could be enclosed on our journey back to Baker Street.

Holmes had telegraphed Mrs. Hudson to advise her of our return, and a substantial fire warmed our sitting room as we embraced the comforts of home once again.

After depositing my luggage in my bedroom, I immediately took to the sideboard for a warm snifter of brandy. Our ever-resourceful landlady informed us that dinner would be served at seven-thirty and handed Holmes several messages.

He sifted through them quickly, discarding any that were not relevant to our current case, relegating some to the jackknife holding his correspondence to the mantle over the fireplace and others into the fire itself.

He dropped into his basket chair and studied the remaining missives carefully. A series of 'hums' and an 'ah ha!' were intermingled with notes he jotted down. At last he sprang from the chair, wrapped himself in an overcoat, muffler and homburg and made for the door.

"Watson, I am off to the Yard. Don't wait up. You must continue your recuperation with a good night's sleep."

As he opened the door he nearly bowled over Mrs. Hudson who was bringing in our dinner. He grabbed her by the shoulders to steady her and declared, "Feed the good doctor, Mrs. Hudson. I shall have mine as a cold supper later," and was off, bounding down the stairs.

She looked down after him, "Hmmf, cold indeed, for I'll not be stayin' up 'til all hours to warm it up again."

Looking at me she smiled and said, "Now, Doctor, Mr. Holmes wrote me of your illness and I have prepared a nice mild stew for you. It should be quite easy to digest and will warm you up as well."

I thanked her and promptly sat down to a delicious dinner. The meals served by Mrs. Raper and Mrs. O'Reilly had been very good, but there was still nothing like the home-cooking of Mrs. Hudson in our Baker Street sitting room.

Half an hour later, I was enjoying another brandy and considering what to read before turning in early. Our efficient landlady came up to clear the dishes and presented me with a note.

"For you, Doctor, it arrived this afternoon. As it was marked 'private' and in a nice lady's hand, I supposed that you might wish to receive it outside the presence of our consulting detective."

I had not seen the handwriting in many years, but considering recent events, I hoped that my memory was correct when it brought forth the name 'Adelaide'.

I was rewarded for my positive thoughts, when it did indeed turn out to be from my newly restored friend. Before reading anything other than the signature, I enquired of Mrs. Hudson, "Did you send back any reply with the messenger?"

"Aye, Doctor, I told the young man that you weren't expected until late this evening or tomorrow," she answered and bustled herself off down the stairs.

I sat by the fire and set down my brandy snifter, which was still nearly half full of the amber liquid, and proceeded to read Adelaide's tidings.

Chapter Twenty-Eight

My Dearest John,

I hope this note finds you well. I have missed you terribly these past few days. Is that so strange? I find that, even though the years have flown by us, without so much as a passing thought, our reunion has stirred such feelings that I can hardly express them. Or perhaps I dare not express them, for fear of being guilty of what may be no more than a school-girl crush. Perhaps something I read of Freud would explain it, a middle-age fear of stagnation, or even death, which causes one to re-examine one's life. I hope my feelings are more than that and, dare I hope, that yours are as well?

Whatever the cause, my dear friend, I find my thoughts turning more and more toward you and this has led to a disruption in my family circle. While George seems to welcome our friendship, Marina has suddenly become contentious and disrespectful. I'm not sure what it is, about you and me, or even if it is us, that is causing this behaviour. I am hoping that you can come and visit, so that I may discuss the matter with you. We shall be at the Langham until Monday next. You have always shown my family such kindness, John, I hope that I may prevail upon you once more.

With love in my heart,

Adelaide

Well, there it was, her thoughts, so parallel to mine, in black and white. I ran my finger over her signature. 'Are we just two middle-aged folk, yearning for the passions of youth, my dear?' I wondered aloud.

I sighed and sipped my brandy, its warmth dispelling the chill that threatened to send me into a relapse of my recent illness. I re-read the letter and then moved to my writing desk. As I wrote out my reply, I found my mind wandering. This very desk was where I had penned the adventures which made Sherlock Holmes a household name. For my own small parts in his cases, I, too, had become somewhat recognized around and about London, if not as much for my participation as for my skill at recording the events. But this was a place where I had mostly written of events that had already occurred. It was an altar to the past. Could it also be a monument to my future? Was it my destiny to be Holmes' Boswell and nothing more? Was my all too short a time with Mary the only respite that Fate would allow? The only complete happiness I would ever know?

Now I found myself sitting there to write a missive that could prove to be a key to a new future. A key that would unlock the chains that bound me to Sherlock Holmes. It was not a binding that I resented. For all his faults, Holmes was the best friend that I could have asked for. I had meant what I said on his birthday, when I told him that I would not have traded our two decades together for anything.

Yet, it was in the course of our affiliation that I had first met Adelaide Savage and now, once again, my alliance with Holmes had brought her back into my life.

I noted a small key fob in a bowl on the desktop amongst other bits and pieces from previous cases, and I recollected him saying at the time, 'I do not take coincidences at face value, Watson'. Before the echo of that recollection rang, I knew at once what I must do.

Ten minutes later, Mrs. Hudson knocked on our sitting room door and poked her head in. As I turned to her I could see young Billy, our part-time pageboy, behind her, all bundled up as if to go out in the snow.

"Begging your pardon, Doctor," she entreated "Is your answer ready for Billy to take?"

I looked at her in numb astonishment, for I had just signed and sealed it. Wordlessly I walked over and handed it to the boy.

"Mrs. Adelaide Savage, the Langham Hotel," I said, somewhat redundantly, for I had written all that on the envelope.

He took it and slipped it deep inside his inner coat pocket to protect it against the weather and started to turn. This act of treating the letter with such care snapped me out of my stupor.

"Wait! Here's money for cab fare," I cried, as I retrieved several coins from my pocket and handed them over.

He accepted them with a smile and was off like a shot, taking the stairs two at a time. I looked at Mrs. Hudson who merely smiled at me and said, "Can I do anything else for you, Doctor?"

I looked down into her twinkling blue eyes, and her all-knowing pixie-like smile and said, "Yes, you can come in and have a drink with me and explain yourself."

I closed the door so that she could not retreat and thus she acquiesced to my demand.

Sitting near the fire I poured her a small sherry and sat opposite her. She took a sip and visibly relaxed, her landlady facade slipping away and the kindly friend overtaking her features.

"Whatever do you mean, Doctor?" she finally asked, with feigned innocence.

I, too, relaxed and slowly lit up a cigar, this one a particularly mild vanilla blend, in light of my tender throat.

"I mean, how did you know that I would answer that message tonight, and that I would be ready to send it at that particular moment?"

She looked into her glass and gave a small laugh, a delightful sound which I had witnessed far too infrequently in our association with her.

She looked toward the ceiling and I could not be sure if her face was shining due to the light above or her own light within. Returning her gaze to me she replied.

"Doctor, Doctor, Doctor," she said, patiently. "Did you not think I would notice, when a man who has lived under my roof for fifteen of the last nineteen years, was in love?"

"Confound it, woman!" I said, in quiet exasperation. "First Holmes and now you! Does everyone know my feelings except for me?"

"I'm surprised Mr. Holmes noticed. He's usually so focused on his cases," she pondered. "But I imagine he 'deduced' it, as he likes to say.

"I may be no detective," she continued, "but I've got eyes, and my woman's intuition is quite intact."

She set down her empty glass and stood. I rose with her, looking into a face that took on a combination of love and wisdom. She placed her strong hand on my arm and looked me in the eye.

"You listen to me, John Hamish Watson. Your Mary was as sweet a creature as to ever walk this earth, no doubt about it. But she is seven years gone. If the Good Lord has given you a second chance at happiness you must not dismiss it lightly."

She nodded her head, as if that was that, and strode for the door. As she turned the handle I called out, "You still haven't told me how you knew when to come for my return message."

She looked back at me with that impish smile again and said, "Oh, that? That was just a **coincidence**." She then winked and drifted out the door, leaving me to my brandy, cigar and pondering thoughts.

Chapter Twenty-Nine

It seems that I fell asleep while reading, for I was awoken by the sound of the clock striking ten. I rubbed my eyes against the light and yawned. Noting the time I rose, put the book back on the shelf and threw a couple of logs on the fire to keep the room warm for Holmes' return.

As I started for my bedroom, suddenly my friend himself burst through the door.

"Ah, Watson, still awake!" said he.

"I was just on my way to bed, Holmes," I yawned.

"Then I shall not keep you, Doctor," he replied, sitting at the writing desk and scratching out a message on a telegraph form. "May I just ask if you are free tomorrow?"

"I have plans for the morning," I answered. "The rest of the day is still open."

"Splendid!" he declared. "I believe you will wish to accompany me tomorrow afternoon to see our case through."

"You've solved it?"

"As our client might say, I shall not count my chickens yet," he said, as he set down his pen.

"I shall be out and about quite early, Watson. Give my regards to Mrs. Savage and I shall see you for lunch perhaps."

Sleepily I started to turn toward my bedroom door when his words broke through and I stared back at him.

"How did you know I was going to see Adelaide tomorrow?"

"Watson, old friend, your feelings have been quite clear and you have been away from her for four days. It is only natural that you should desire to renew your visits. Besides, there is a distinct odour of her perfume lingering here at the desk. You have, no doubt, received a message from her and have replied this very evening."

I pulled Adelaide's letter from my pocket and sniffed it. There was a hint of her perfume but nothing more. It was not scented paper, merely the faint aroma of lilac that was the basis of her favourite fragrance.

"Holmes," I demanded, waving the letter in the air, "how on earth could you detect the scent? The paper lay there for less than fifteen minutes, more than two hours ago!"

"My olfactory senses are much keener than yours, Doctor," he replied. "And I've not had my sinuses invaded by a cold, as you have."

He stood and started across the room, "Good night, Watson. I'm going down to retrieve what I can of my supper."

I watched him whisk out the door and shook my head. Sleep was going to be a welcome distraction.

*****

The next morning I was up at eight o'clock. While I was enjoying porridge, toast and coffee, a messenger arrived with a note for me. I opened it and found it unsigned, but I knew who it was from.

I copied it down, burned the original and left my version for Holmes. I had promised Maury the Bagger, that I would not reveal him as my source and did not want his handwriting recognized or analyzed by the great detective.

I went 'round to see Mr. Alston and found him much recovered. He met me in his sitting room and stood to shake my hand as I entered.

"Bless you, Dr. Watson. I am feeling my old self again. Your ministrations have beaten back my influenza."

He returned to his chair and I checked his pulse and looked into his eyes and throat. "No more coughing?" I asked

"Not a peep since Wednesday," he replied

"Do you feel at all winded going up and down the stairs?"

"Not a bit, sir. I tell you I am cured and I thank you for it!"

"There is no cure for influenza, Mr. Alston," I replied. "I merely treated the symptoms and your body did the rest. Fortunately, your constitution is quite strong for a man your age. I should say, that if the storm breaks and we're not facing a blizzard, you can go back to your office on Monday."

"Where I shall write you a sizable check for your services, sir."

"That's not necessary. You know my standard fee. That will be quite sufficient."

"Very well," he answered, not very enthusiastically. "May I at least offer you some tea before you go?"

"That is most kind of you, sir, but I have another appointment to keep and I should be on my way."

"Well, thank you for coming by, Doctor," he stood, shaking my hand again before I ventured once more out into the chilly morning air.

The snow had stopped falling, but there was sufficient evidence of its passing for children to build small snowmen and have snowball fights in the street. One particularly well-rounded spheroid took off my bowler just as I was about to step up into my cab. I turned to the sound of laughter and screaming children as they ran away. I smiled as I stooped to retrieve my hat and brush it off, remembering the same prank that I had performed as a child. I had an excellent arm, even as a youth and, while I preferred rugby, I was a proficient bowler in my younger days.

Boarding the cab, I called out 'Langham Hotel' to the driver and sat back to contemplate what the next hour might bring.

The fleeting thoughts of my youth as a cricketer decided to return to my mind. I reflected on my college days and the ladies I have known then and since, over many nations and three continents. Some were infatuations, some unrequited love, some short-term passions that quickly burned out. Only Mary had ever truly held my heart.

Could Adelaide be to me what Mary had been? Would it even be fair to expect that of her? The cab's horses slid on the icy road, then they caught themselves as the driver attempted to brake. Finally, we lurched to a stop and I found myself at the Langham. The jolt shook me out of my mental debate and made me remember what Holmes had said about overanalyzing. I also thought back to Mrs. Hudson's words of the previous night and decided it was time to follow my heart.

I took the lift up to the floor where this adventure had begun. I was five minutes early but could not restrain myself and knocked on the door to the Savage's suite.

It was opened by George. The young man was looking very fine indeed, in one of his new suits for school.

"Oh, hello, Dr. Watson," he said. "I was just about to step down the hall and call upon Miss Clemens. Have you been to see her?"

"I did not realize she had returned from Reading," I replied. "I shall certainly stop over and check on her before I leave."

"Come in, and have a seat. I'll let Mother know you're here."

I entered and took to the sofa, where I could enjoy the warmth of the fire. George came back out quickly and said his mother would be out in a minute and stood by the fire himself, somewhat nervously.

As much to steady my own nerves as his, I engaged him in conversation.

"Your suit fits you well, George. That latest style should make you fit right in at the university. Are you all set to start?"

"Yes, Doctor," he answered. "I've all my clothes and supplies and have already met some of my fellow-students. I'll be moving in over the weekend."

"Well, that's fine," I replied. "If you should need anything while you're here in London do not hesitate to call on me."

"That's very kind of you, Doctor. I shall remember that."

He hesitated, as if unsure how to ask his next question, so he made a statement instead.

"I appreciate your kindness toward Mother as well. I haven't seen her so happy since my father died."

I cleared my throat and replied, "Your mother is a remarkable woman, George, running the estate and raising the two of you by herself. You should be proud of her and proud to be her son."

"Oh, I am sir," he declared. "I was just wondering about how she'll get along while I'm away at college and, if you'll beg my pardon, sir, if you and she ..."

Before he could finish that question, Adelaide swept into the room with Marina in tow.

Chapter Thirty

"George Clarkson Savage," she exclaimed, "that's enough ! Leave Dr. Watson's private business to himself."

"Sorry, Mother," he said, chagrined. "Excuse me, Dr. Watson I didn't mean to embarrass you."

"Nonsense, lad," I said, standing upon Adelaide's entrance, "You are the man of the house. You've every right to question a suitor's intentions."

"John!" Adelaide interjected.

"No, Adelaide," I answered. "He is of an age where he has responsibilities to you, and looking out for your well-being should be a primary concern for him. You should be proud of his love and concern for you."

"George," I said in all earnestness as I turned to look him in the eye. "I do not know where this friendship between your mother and me may lead. But when, or if, it takes on a role of courtship or engagement, I shall ensure that you and Marina know and, I sincerely hope, approve."

I believe, at that moment, George Savage matured by several years before our eyes. He stood a little straighter, his countenance took on that of a proper English gentleman and in all seriousness, he held out his hand for me to shake.

"Dr. Watson, I thank you," he said, and I believe his voice even deepened in that instant as his grip matched my own. "I shall broach the matter no more until I hear from you." He turned and looked at his mother, in whose eyes I saw tears. "Except to say that, should the time come, I would be proud to be your stepson. Now if you will excuse me, I am late for my visit to Miss Clemens."

He gave his mother a kiss on the cheek and his sister a look which I could not decipher. Upon his exit Adelaide wiped her eyes with her kerchief and we all sat down again. She and Marina took the sofa and I accepted a chair across from them.

Marina is a beautiful young lady with a trim figure, long brown hair, a heart-shaped face and large green eyes. She was wearing a royal blue dress with white trim at the cuffs and collar.

Adelaide was wearing dark green with an open collar. Her hair was up, parted down the middle with her blonde curls framing the sides of her face and a braided bun tied up in the back.

"John," she began, blushing and then paused, trying to collect thoughts from what must have been a whirlwind in her mind. "I ... I hardly know what to say. This is certainly not how I imagined our conversation going."

"In all my years of association with Sherlock Holmes," I stated, "I have observed, and tried to learn, the manner of taking whatever actions or conversation comes my way and adapting my reaction to it, in spite of preconceived notions. It is not always easy, and I have failed a number of times, I assure you. But in this instance I merely allowed my heart to do the talking. I meant every word I said, Adelaide."

She held an open palm to her chest, "My goodness ..."

"Mother, let me get you some tea, would you like some, Doctor?" Marina offered, her face soft and pleasant and far different from the impatient young lady she had appeared when last I saw her.

"Yes, thank you, that would be nice, one lump of sugar please, Marina" I answered.

She gracefully departed to that portion of the suite reserved for food preparation.

Adelaide wiped her eyes again and said, "I was hoping that your feelings matched my own, John. I have always cherished your friendship from when you and Mr. Holmes saved us from losing our home. These past few days have re-kindled feelings in me that I haven't known since before poor Victor took to his drug habit."

I moved to her side and took her hands in mine. "Then we must not let these feelings fall by the wayside, for I too, have felt a joy that I haven't known since my poor Mary."

"I know how much you loved her, John. Frankly, I didn't know if I could, or even should, try to compete with her memory."

"Look at me, Adelaide," I implored. She turned and faced me so that we became enveloped in each other's eyes.

"Mary and Victor are gone. As Mrs. Hudson advised me last night, we shouldn't limit ourselves to only one chance in a lifetime at happiness, if a second one comes along.

"Therefore, Mrs. Savage," I stated in a formal tone. "When you return to your estates I should like permission to call upon you as your friend and let us see where our time together leads us."

Responding to my playful mood she replied, "Dr. Watson, I accept your proposal."

"Mother!" cried Marina, who was just walking in with the tea tray. She set it down quickly before she dropped it and rushed to her mother's side to give her a hug.

"Marina, darling, wait," her mother implored. "It's not what you think!"

"Marina!" I said, but then I found myself in her embrace.

"Oh, Doctor, it's wonderful!" she cried.

Finally, I was able to pull away and take her gently by the shoulders, "Marina, hold on, come, sit down."

I guided her gently down onto the sofa next to her mother.

"Now then, the 'proposal' your mother accepted is that I would like to call upon her at your home from time to time, to see if our friendship blossoms into something more. Marriage is not something one rushes into after so little time spent together."

"Oh," she replied blushing, "I'm so sorry, Doctor."

She turned at looked at her mother, "After our talk last night I thought ..."

"Hush!" declared Adelaide. "The Doctor is right and I am delighted at the proposition."

"Wait a minute," came back her daughter, with determination in her eyes. "I read *The Sign of the Four*. You proposed to Mary the fourth time you saw her. You had only spent a few hours together. You've known Mother for years."

Trapped by my own words, I could only stammer, "But that was different, I ..." and I could think of nothing to say.

Fortunately, her mother came to my rescue, "Marina," she said, taking her daughter's hand. "John was a very lucky man when he found Mary. Most often 'love at first sight' is rarely true love. The path he and I are about to embark on is far more likely to succeed. True lovers should be best friends first. Looks can fade, physical abilities diminish, but true friendship lasts. That's what love must be based upon."

"Yes," I agreed, relieved and impressed. "Quite right, well put, Adelaide."

"Now can we have some tea?" asked the mother to her daughter.

Marina poured and we all sat back and sipped in enjoyment.

"My goodness," Adelaide suddenly declared. "I completely forgot about why I asked you to come."

"Yes?" I replied, setting down my cup at the prospect of this new turn of conversation.

"Marina has something to say to you," she announced.

The young woman, already embarrassed by her earlier outburst, bowed her head sheepishly.

"It seems so silly now, Mother," she murmured.

"Nevertheless, we agreed," Adelaide stated, resolutely.

Marina let out a sigh and proceeded. "I owe you an apology, Doctor. My behaviour the other night was atrociously rude and I am sorry."

I folded my hands in my lap, not quite sure how to respond. As occasionally happens however, my mouth worked faster than my brain.

"I accept your apology, Marina," I said, then, realizing how pompous that sounded, I added, "Was there something bothering you? Is there anything I can do for you?"

She smiled, "Not now, Doctor. By expressing your desire to visit mother at home you have solved what I thought was going to be a problem."

I was confused and said so.

"Apparently," said her mother, "Marina has a young man of her own to whom is anxious to return. She was afraid I was going to extend my stay in London because you and I were getting along so well,"

"Well," I replied, "we can't have that. Who is this lucky young man who seems to have stolen your heart?"

"Joshua Morgan; his family breeds horses just down the road from us."

"Really? Is he any relation the American who bred the Morgan horse?" I asked.

"If you trace back far enough they did branch off from the same family tree. He is very intelligent, Doctor. He's a graduate of Oxford City Technical School and he practically runs the family farm."

"And," chimed in Adelaide, "he has apparently been paying a lot of attention to Marina at church and local social events. I was aware of his presence in her circle of friends, but it was only last night that I learned how deeply her feelings ran toward him."

"I miss him, Doctor," responded Marina. "It's enough that I will miss church services with him this Sunday. I was afraid this trip would be prolonged even more because of you. I'm sorry I was so selfish. I did not take Mother's feelings into consideration at all. I had no idea she could feel for you what I feel for Joshua."

Adelaide gave a small laugh and smiled at me, "I explained to her that feelings do not diminish with age, John. Indeed, under the right circumstances they can be stronger than ever."

I returned her smile with one of equal joy, "Well, I'm glad we've got all that settled."

We sat, drank our tea and talked more about less weighty topics until the clock struck eleven.

209

"I really should go see Miss Clemens," I conceded. "And Holmes desires my presence this afternoon. He is quite close to solving our case."

"Then you must go, John," replied Adelaide, as we all stood up together.

Marina came to me and gave me a kiss on the cheek. "Good day, Doctor. I shall look forward to your visits from now on."

She then left the room, discreetly leaving her mother and me alone.

We walked to the door together, her hand slipping around my arm.

"Whatever Mr. Holmes has planned, you promise me you'll be careful?"

"Our case has posed little danger thus far," I answered. "But I will take appropriate precautions. If we wrap things up, as Holmes believes, would you care to join me for dinner tomorrow evening?"

"I should be delighted, Doctor," she cooed, inclining her head toward me.

At the door we faced each other. I started to speak then thought better of it. This was no time for words. Instead I took her in my arms and our lips melted into a long, lingering kiss.

Chapter Thirty-One

Five minutes later, having bid Adelaide adieu, I was knocking on Clemens' door.

Olivia Clemens opened the door and smiled when she saw me.

"Dr. Watson, do come in," she said, "I'll get Sam."

"I welcome his company, Mrs. Clemens, but I really came to check on Jean. I understand she is with you now?"

"Oh yes, that nice young man, George, is here with her in the sitting room, come I'll take you."

She escorted me to that same room wherein our adventure had begun with the theft of Clemens' papers. George's new found maturity seemed to put him at ease in the company of the attractive Miss Clemens, something I would not have thought possible of the shy young lad that I had introduced her to at the theatre. He stood in all his good manners when Olivia entered the room. He shook my hand, not quite knowing what else he should do, since it would appear rude not to do so.

"Hello again, Doctor," he said. "Did all go well with Marina and Mother?"

"Yes, George, Marina was a particularly interesting participant in our conversation. I'm glad we resolved her issues."

"I should have told Mother months ago," he admitted. "But Marina made me promise not to. I did keep a discreet eye on her though. Just to make sure things stayed above board."

"As a good brother should," I answered. "Now, Miss Clemens, how are you feeling?"

"Much better, Doctor, thank you."

"Any headaches or tingling sensations?"

"A slight headache when I awoke this morning, but it left after I ate breakfast."

211

"I'd like to just check your pulse and temperature, if I may? "

"I really feel fine, Doctor," she answered, not wishing to be subjected to an examination in front of her guest, no doubt.

George must have sensed her hesitancy and spoke up, "You should do as the doctor says, Jean. I'll wait in the other room, if that's all right with you, Mrs. Clemens?"

I looked at Olivia and added, "I'll only be two or three minutes."

She acquiesced and George stepped out. I retrieved my thermometer from my bag and took her pulse as it measured her temperature. When I retrieved it she was exactly at 98.6. Her pulse however, was rather high, and I said so.

"Your temperature is fine but your pulse is up a bit."

I then lowered my voice, "It may only be from the company you're keeping," I said, giving a glance at the room where George stood by, "but you should keep resting and not exert yourself."

I looked at her mother, "Let me know if the headaches continue, or if there is any sign of tingling or numbness. Should she have another episode you should get her to hospital immediately, even if it passes quickly."

"Thank you, Doctor," she replied.

"And you, young lady," I ordered, "rest, make sure you eat well and drink hot fluids."

She let out a sigh, "All right, Doctor. Thank you for your concern."

"My duty as a physician and a friend of the family," I replied.

Passing through the room where George awaited as I left, I found the lad engaged in conversation with Sam Clemens, who was offering him a cigar.

I could see the hesitancy in George's face, not wishing to insult the father of a girl he cared about. I decided to come to his rescue.

"Now, George, no cigars for you until you are completely healed from your cold. I don't want to have to treat that throat all over again."

He looked at me and hesitated for a split second before recognition of my ploy gleamed in his eye. Fortunately the American author was also looking my way and did not notice.

"I'm afraid he's right, Mr. Clemens. I really shouldn't."

"I'm all finished with Jean, if you'd like to go back in."

Nodding in grateful acknowledgement he excused himself and returned to the ladies.

"How about you, Doc? Care to join me in a smoke?" Clemens proffered the cigar toward me.

"Thank you, no, Sam. I myself am just recovering from a sore throat. I should not be out in the cold today if I didn't have patients to look in on. Have you ever thought of cutting back on those? Too much tobacco can be harmful."

"You know, Doc, I've quit many a time ... for two or three hours. I remember when I was a lad of fifteen and a preacher feller told me I could live ten years longer if I didn't smoke. Well, I vowed on the spot to quit, to abstain from the noxious habit forever. Then an hour went by, then another hour, which must have been at least 75 minutes long. And then a third hour, which I swear, by all that is blessed, must have lasted at least 97 minutes. Finally I just went and lit up the biggest cigar in my poke and commenced to blowing smoke rings for all I was worth.

"Now that preacher feller happened to come by as I was a smokin' like a chimney and cried out, 'Tarnation, Samuel, couldn't you quit smoking for even one afternoon ?'

"Well, Doc I just looked straight at him, blew out the biggest puff o' smoke I could muster and says to him, 'The way I figured it out, Preacher, is that if I got to live an extra decade without being able to enjoy my tobacco, it just wasn't worth it."

I smiled as he chomped on his stogie and grinned. "Be that as it may, Sam, there have been studies in medical journals that prove smoking should only be done in moderation."

"Let me tell you somethin', Doc," he said, pointing his cigar at me for emphasis. "You should never read medical journals or health books. You could die because of a misprint."

I laughed out loud at this remark and began coughing because my throat really was still sore.

"Take it easy there, Doc. Here, take swig of this." He produced a hip flask, opened it and handed it to me. I gave it a whiff and took a tentative sip. It was delicious and marvellously soothing as it tickled my throat.

"This is very good, Sam. What is it?"

"A particular favourite of mine," he replied. "It's a soda fountain drink called Coca Cola. The feller that invented it claims it can cure a whole hospital full of diseases, including dyspepsia, headache, morphine addiction, and even impotence."[1]

I looked sceptical. "I know there has been much praise for various soda waters, but that seems a little exaggerated."

"Oh, I've no doubt, but it tastes mighty fine all the same," he replied, taking a healthy swig himself. Then he capped it and looked at me.

"Now, tell me, how is Mr. Sherlock Holmes coming on my case?"

I did not want to instil false hopes so I tempered my answer.

"He has eliminated a few suspects and is narrowing the field," I replied. "We just returned to London last night. I am going to meet him now to see what answers he derived from his sources this morning. Have you heard from anyone?"

"Not a peep, Doc," he answered. "Whoever took them papers of mine seems to have no interest in selling them back. I may have to resign myself to writing my memoirs from memory. Which is always a tricky thing, being so favourable to the rememberer at the expense of the true facts.

"I'm sure they will be entertaining all the same," I replied, discreetly stepping toward the door.

---

[1] At this point in time Coca Cola still included cocaine in its formula.

He stepped along with me and put a hand on my shoulder "Well hopefully Holmes is as good as you've made him out to be in your tales."

"He has had a remarkable success rate," I responded, as I shook the hand he held out, and we said our 'goodbyes'.

I found a cab quickly, for the weather was too cold and threatening for walking. I was back in Baker Street just as the snow started to fall again, warming myself by the fire when Inspector Hopkins arrived.

Chapter Thirty-Two

After Mrs. Hudson showed the harried-looking Scotland Yarder up the stairs, I offered him a seat by the fire and a brandy to warm his insides.

"I assume Holmes is expecting you, Inspector?" I asked as I poured his drink.

"Yes, Doctor," he answered. "He asked me to bring my findings on certain persons and meet him here at half past noon."

"Which persons?" I queried.

His answer was interrupted by Holmes bursting into the room.

"Aha, Hopkins, you have it?" he demanded.

"Here, Mr. Holmes," he replied, standing and retrieving a large brown envelope from his inner coat pocket.

The detective tore it open and scanned its contents quickly.

"I'm afraid there's not much there," apologized Hopkins.

"Yes, I see, Inspector," Holmes intoned in all seriousness. Then, unexpectedly, he smiled.

"What? What is it, Holmes?" I beseeched of him, as I also stood and attempted to glance over his shoulder. He quickly folded them back up.

"In and of themselves these papers are quite worthless," he said, waving them in the air. "However the information was necessary to my elimination of suspects."

Turning to Hopkins he added, "Thank you for your efforts, Inspector, I shall keep you apprised."

"Mr. Holmes," said Hopkins unhappily, "My superiors are pressing for me to arrest Hodges. They believe the

217

evidence of his shoeprint, and the fact that he is a fellow American with a rival publishing company is sufficient to hold him."

Holmes smiled at him, "Quite so. I should not waste any time in arresting Hodges," he said.

"Then he is our man after all?" said the Scotland Yard Inspector, breathing a sigh of relief.

"That is not what I said," replied Holmes, calmly stuffing his pipe with tobacco from the Persian slipper hanging from the corner of the fireplace mantle.

"What do mean, sir?"

"I mean I should not waste any time arresting Hodges without knowing where the papers are."

"But, if he is our man we can make him talk!"

"And risk an international incident and the ire of the press? I think not," Holmes replied.

"Then, what do you recommend, Mr. Holmes?" demanded the Inspector, exasperated.

Lighting his churchwarden, Holmes advised, "Give me twenty-four hours, Inspector. I believe by that time I shall either have the papers in hand or know where they are. Then you will be free to act."

"Very well, Mr. Holmes," said Hopkins, as he donned his hat. "You've helped us at the Yard often enough for me to trust your judgment. I shall expect to hear from you by tomorrow afternoon then."

The inspector left us and I turned back to Holmes, who now sat in his basket chair, quietly smoking. I took to my chair and retrieved my brandy from the table.

"So?" I asked

In answer he tossed the envelope of papers from Hopkins across to me. I snatched them out of the air with my free hand and set my glass down to open the envelope.

I scanned the papers quickly and found nothing of consequence except surprise at their identities. I looked up at my companion who merely smiled and kept puffing on his pipe.

I re-read the papers, this time with much more care, looking for any possible reference that might connect them to our case. Still finding none, I held them up toward him and said "What is it, Holmes? There is nothing here, just biographical information on two distinguished gentlemen, at that. Surely you don't suspect them of stealing Clemens' papers?"

"Don't I?" he smiled, enigmatically. Then he noticed the note I had left on the table. "What's this?" he asked as he crossed to pick it up.

"Information you requested from our mutual acquaintance," I replied. "Is it significant?"

"Watson," he smiled, "let me join you in a drink and then we shall ring up Mrs. Hudson for lunch. This is final confirmation of my hypothesis and, I believe, guarantees we shall make good on my promise to Hopkins."

"How is that information possibly significant?" I implored.

"I shall reveal all to you later this afternoon, my friend. For now I suggest a healthy lunch and for you a nap to restore your strength. The after effects of your illness have not completely left you and you will want your full wits about you where we are going."

"Why? Where are we going?"

He actually grinned as he said, "The Diogenes Club."

Chapter Thirty-Three

Holmes was silent as our cab crunched its way through the slush-covered streets en route to Pall Mall, just as the sun was beginning to set. After all our years together, I knew better than to try to penetrate his thoughts to satisfy my own curiosity. Although I knew that he occasionally frequented the reclusive club, founded by his brother Mycroft, I myself had only been there under those rare circumstances when Holmes was summoned by, or consulting, his older brother.

The Diogenes Club is named for the ancient Greek philosopher Diogenes of Sinope, better known as Diogenes the Cynic. He was noted for carrying a lamp about in the daytime, claiming to be looking for an honest man. The Club is housed in a three storey, grey block structure, with hints of Grecian architecture framing its doorway and windows. The doors are dark English walnut with brass fittings and no windows, save those framed above the opening itself. There are secondary storm doors of black solid steel which can be closed over the walnut enhanced entrance, to ward off unwanted visitors during those rare hours that the club is closed.

Snow still clung to the tops of the window frames. The stairway to the entrance and the stair railings had been swept and brushed clean. No address number or name plaque announces the existence of the facility. Its anonymity is one of the chief attractions for its exclusive membership.

A warm glow appeared through the windows above the door. Upon entering, we found the inside well-lit against the outer gloom by a large chandelier casting its electric beams over a stately lobby. High above, the skylight dome was still half covered in snow, admitting what little sun penetrated the clouds.

There are only two places within this bastion of exclusivity where speech is allowed. The Strangers' Room is one, where members can meet for quiet discussion; and here, where we stood in the lobby, announcing our names to the attendant. As he took our overcoats, hats and umbrellas, I noted that this man, though attired in typical butler's garb, was young and well-built, with the bearing of a soldier. He informed us Mycroft was awaiting our arrival in the aforementioned room. We immediately ascended the stairs to that locale to find him sitting at a table, near a window overlooking the grey-streaked street below.

Being seven years his brother's senior, Mycroft had gone completely grey, in both the mane of hair that receded back from his wide forehead and the mutton chop whiskers that swept across his ample cheeks.

As we approached, Mycroft remained seated, greeting us simply by name and waving to other seats at the table. I let Holmes choose his chair first, knowing that occasionally he preferred to observe his subject from specific angles and in certain lighting.

"So, Sherlock," stated the elder Holmes "What can I do for you today?"

"You obviously were expecting me," the younger brother stated. "You should know what I want."

"If you would, please verify."

"Ward James." answered my companion simply.

I snapped my head around to look at him, aghast. Mycroft merely smirked and put on a fatherly air. "So, you believe you've eliminated the impossible?"

"Yes."

"Does not Mr. James represent the improbable then?"

"I believe he represents you, dear brother. Or that you know who does control his actions."

"To what actions do you refer?"

"Really, Mycroft, is this game necessary? Mr. James broke in and stole the private papers of a foreign visitor. It is a typical tactic of the British Intelligence Service, to which he is connected, as I daresay, are you."

This revelation startled me. I had come to know over the years that Mycroft held a key government post. In the adventure I had recorded, but not yet published, as *The Bruce Partington Plans*, which had occurred just five years before, I had assumed that Mycroft was involved at the behest of the Prime Minister. He appeared to be merely a go-between to engage his younger brother. I should have known better. Holmes at the time had stated, 'Mycroft *is* the British government at times.' His great brain was a connecting point for various government policies and actions. He could predict outcomes and consequences to such a degree that he had become indispensable. But to accuse him of what we were investigating as a crime seemed outlandish.

"Holmes," I asked incredulously, "how can you suspect that British Intelligence would be involved in the theft of Clemens' papers? Are you saying that he is an American spy?"

"No dear fellow," my friend answered, "Although his travels and connections would make a good cover story, he has not the personality to succeed at such an occupation. He does, however, write down nearly everything he sees." The detective looked pointedly at his brother "And it is my conviction that something he may have written down is embarrassing to someone in high circles."

Mycroft sighed resignedly.

"**Embarrassing?**" I queried. "Not some important military information that he may have stumbled across by accident?"

"No," replied the younger Holmes, "Were it anything of importance, Clemens could have been approached openly and appealed to as an American citizen and thus an ally of England. It stands to reason that whatever information he may possess is something that is personally sensitive and not a national security issue. Therefore, it may be interpreted by

Clemens to be open game for publication under his American ideals of freedom of the press. What say you, Mycroft?"

The leonine head of Mycroft Holmes had turned to gaze out at the snow. His massive hands were folded on the table while his shoulders hunched as if he could draw that head in like a turtle. Were it possible for a Holmes to show emotion, I would have stated that a trace of embarrassment had imperceptibly manifested itself as a blink of an eye on that otherwise impassive face.

Turning back toward us he glanced at me and then gazed at his brother.

"It is a deplorable use of government resources." he grumbled.

"I can only think of two people who could influence you to such an action." replied Holmes.

"I can assure you it is not the behest of the Sovereign," remarked Mycroft.

"Salisbury then."[1]

"The Prime Minister?" I questioned.

"No matter!" Mycroft replied with a wave off of his hand. "The information that was feared is not among Clemens' notes. I will have them sent 'round to Baker Street in the morning and you may return them to your American friend. Make up what story you will, so long as the government participation is not mentioned."

My companion seemed to take this in stride. Perhaps because of his intimate knowledge of his brother, he was willing to acquiesce to this condition.

I, on the other hand, was incensed.

"This is outrageous, Mr. Holmes." I cried, ignoring the restraining hand of my friend. "Taking such liberties may be well and good against criminals and spies, but to invade the privacy of upstanding citizens of any country is against the foundations of British law. I am shocked that you could be involved in such activities!"

---

[1] Prime Minister Robert Gascoyne-Cecil, 3rd Marquess of Salisbury.

Mycroft stared back with those steely grey eyes and asked, "Do you recall your Dickens, Doctor?"

"What has Dickens to do with anything?" I replied coldly. But next to me, the younger Holmes was on the verge of a smirk.

"A Tale of Two Cities, sir;" continued Mycroft, "'The needs of the many outweigh the needs of the few, or the one'. Some youthful indiscretions, which were committed in the presence of Mr. Clemens many years ago, could curtail the career of a future British statesman should they be published. As it happens, there is no mention of them in his papers so they can be returned intact."

"Why not just ask him not to print the story?" I shot back, unwilling to let it go.

The voice of my friend interceded. "Because, Watson, if the data were not recorded, there was no need to rekindle Mr. Clemens memory of the incident."

"Sherlock, you are showing a remarkable understanding of the political games that must be played." Mycroft replied.

"Tut, tut, dear Brother." Holmes said, clicking his tongue. "I may be understanding, but I am certainly not in agreement. It is only for your sake that I will do as you ask."

"Good enough, Sherlock." He rose to signal the end of our meeting and Holmes and I left him there to return to the warmth of our own fire, which Mrs. Hudson had dutifully kept kindled in our sitting room.

As we returned to Baker Street I queried Holmes on how he came to identify Ward James as the culprit.

"It was as Mycroft inferred, Doctor. Once we eliminated the other possibilities we were left with the certainty that it was a professional job and that no hotel personnel were involved. In addition there was the added factor of misdirection to a point that most professional thieves would not bother to deal with."

"You are referring to the false clues planted in the room and on the fire escape?"

"Yes, Watson, that left us with someone who had to have access to a key or an excellent lock pick set with steady nerves that avoided slips and scratches on the lock.

"Then there was the question of motive. Who would want to stop the publication of Clemens's autobiography and why? Did it have to do with personal, business or some higher cause? Surmising that the government might be involved, I determined to consider James more closely. His obvious military bearing and his physical capability made it possible. His alibi and background story were so thin that it was evident he was not what he seemed, even though our friend Hopkins was satisfied. Thus with all other possibilities eliminated, his involvement, though seemingly improbable, proved to be the truth. I am certain, now, that James committed the theft. He improvised a misdirection when he found Hodges' boots in the hallway and put them on his own smaller feet. This is why the weight distribution was all wrong. After setting the stage, he then lowered the case to his accomplice and friend, Reese, in the alley. They, in turn, passed it on to Sir Edwin Snider, who delivered it to Mycroft when they dropped him off at the Diogenes club that evening."

"That is why you had Hopkins make the enquiries about Sir Edwin and Lord Roseboro ?"

"Yes, old friend. Hopkins' information contained nothing, which is what I expected after I contacted sources at the foreign office to look into their military careers. Any indiscretions of their past were eliminated, yet both seem to have a source of income beyond their estates, particularly Snider, whose lands have fallen on hard times. Both were distinguished soldiers and served together. Each received commendations, some of which were for missions classified as secret.

"So you concluded that they were connected to the British Intelligence Service ?"

"Yes, and with Roseboro's injury, ostensibly in the line of duty, it was no small leap to presume he had enlisted his son to follow in his footsteps. The young man had distinguished himself in Her Majesty's service and had a natural talent for the type of work the Intelligence Service requires. Of course he, in turn, would enlist the assistance of his friend and classmate, Harry Reese, thus explaining Reese's extra income."

"But why did you assume government involvement at all?" I asked.

"The precision of the operation, the targeting of Clemens' papers, even though there were other valuables in the room, and the access to the room itself. Your note from our 'mutual acquaintance' confirmed that the only set of lock picks, outside of the ones you obtained for me and those purchased by licensed locksmiths, were sent to an inconsequential office of the government. The timeline also held enough of a gap for a quick plan of action on James' part."

"But what does Salisbury have to do with this?" I responded.

"Not the Prime Minister, Watson, but likely one of his sons or nephews who need their reputation intact if they are to pursue their own political careers. There are times when even being able to claim 'Bob's your uncle'[2] is not enough to escape public scrutiny."

With that, we arrived at Baker Street. Holmes delved into one of his scientific experiments while I perused the late editions of the daily press.

*****

Over dinner which, due to my mood, did not receive the attention Mrs. Hudson's culinary efforts deserved, I still complained bitterly to Holmes.

"This is simply intolerable, Holmes." I stated, stabbing at a boiled potato. "I don't see how you can let yourself be a party to it."

---

[2] One theory of the origin of the term 'Bob's your uncle' is believed to have come about due to Lord Salisbury, real name Robert Cecil, appointing his nephew, Arthur Balfour, to a succession of government posts. This blatant nepotism contributes to the definition that if 'Bob's your uncle', you will have it easy and can get away with anything.

"There, there, Watson." He replied, lighting his pipe, having finished his meal while I had done most of the talking. "As abhorrent as political gamesmanship is to me, at least in this instance no harm will have been done. Clemens will have his papers returned intact."

"But, what if there **had been** something in them that the government wanted to suppress? What then? Where does one draw the line between government interference and civil liberty? This case could easily have resulted in a denial of freedom of the press. Something your brother seems to fear."

The cherry aroma of his pipe smoke hung in the air, as did my question, for a long moment before he replied.

"I believe it was Thomas Jefferson who said; '… were it left to me to decide whether we should have a government without newspapers, or newspapers without a government, I should not hesitate a moment to prefer the latter.' In this, Watson, I heartily concur, with some reservation. Were all citizens educated and literate, and all newspapers honest and unbiased, then it might be possible for the masses to govern themselves without the bureaucracy that stifles progress today.

"Unfortunately, this is not the case, and I fear governments will always be, for you and I have seen far too much evil in this world to deny their necessity. But we still have the power to make matters at least a little more palatable"

"What do you mean, Holmes? What do you intend to do?" I asked.

"We'll see what the morrow brings, old friend. For now I suggest you finish your excellent meal before it turns into a cold supper."

He retired to his chair by the fire, smoke curling about his head, feet stretched out to the warmth of the blaze and fingers steepled in front of closed eyes as he lost himself in thought.

*****

The next morning, shortly after nine, Mrs. Hudson announced that Mr. Ward James had arrived with a package for Holmes. Asking her to show him up, Holmes stood with his back to the window of our sitting room, after first noting that our visitor had arrived on horseback.

That gentleman entered the room with a large canvas bag. In contrast to his previous appearance, he was dressed in corduroy trousers, a plaid flannel shirt, black flat cap and pea-jacket. His steely blue eyes locked on Holmes' perceptive grey orbs. For a moment they seemed frozen in a staring bout. At last, the younger man looked down to the bag at his side. Like Father Christmas drawing a present from his sack, he withdrew Clemens' overstuffed briefcase and handed it to me.

"I trust all is intact, Lieutenant," said Holmes flatly.

To his credit, the young man barely flinched at this reference to his rank. Had I not been studying him carefully I certainly would have missed it.

"Intact and exactly in the order and condition in which they were received. M's orders."

"Mycroft is thorough," replied Holmes.

"Received?" I spat, "Stolen you mean!"

James turned toward me "Reconnoitred and returned, sir." He turned back to Holmes giving a slight bow and with a 'By your leave' turned toward the door. Holmes interrupted his exit with a final comment.

"You may find it amusing, Mr. James, to know that it was exactly one week ago to this very hour, that Mr. Clemens engaged us on this case."

James smiled, touched his cap in salute and strode purposefully through the door.

I strode to Holmes' side at the window and watched the young man mount his horse and trot off down the street.

"Definitely cavalry," I observed "but how did you know he was a lieutenant?"

"A combination of his age, the responsibility of his assignment and his manner in the presence of his elders. He is new to his rank and still finding his way in the chain of command. Were he a captain or higher that would not be an issue. Even when he is among civilians his youth and military training give him away. If he is to succeed as an agent of

British Intelligence he'll need to learn to throw himself into his role much more convincingly."

"What was that about being engaged on the case for exactly one week?"

Holmes smiled, "Just a reminder of a remark he made while at Roseboro, about how quickly your published cases always seem to be solved."

"So, now what, Holmes?" I asked. "Do we simply return Clemens' papers with no explanation?"

"I doubt our American friend would be satisfied with that," he answered. "No, I am concocting a plausible version of the truth in my mind, without revealing all. I shall send a message to Mr. Clemens and arrange to return his material just before lunch. This will allow us to keep our explanation short with the excuse of having a luncheon engagement of our own to keep, so we cannot be detained long with the many questions I'm sure his journalistic mind will be bursting to ask."

We arrived at the Langham Hotel just after 11:00 a.m. and took the lift to Mr. Clemens' floor. He answered the door himself and invited us in with anticipation. Seeing his briefcase in Holmes grasp he exclaimed with delight, "Mr. Holmes, dare I say you've solved the case? That looks like my satchel."

Holmes replied, handing over the object of our search, "Indeed, Mr. Clemens. I trust you will find your papers intact, but you should go through them all to make sure."

"And the culprit who committed this criminality?" he asked

"Alas, he escaped on horseback after Watson laid hands upon the goods. But rest assured, the British government knows who is responsible and he shall not escape his fate."

The American gentleman turned and shook my hand vigorously, "Thank you, Doc! My memory is not what it was and I'm sure there are things written in here that would have been forgot."

I nodded, embarrassed, "It was really Holmes' doing. I merely was in his company when we confronted the thief and was closest to the case when the man fled."

"Well, thank you both. I shall review the contents over the next few days. Can you join us for lunch?"

Holmes responded in his most gracious manner, "Unfortunately we must be on our way to an appointment on behalf of Lord Salisbury. Have you met the Prime Minister, Mr. Clemens?"

A thoughtful look passed over the aging gentleman's features, "I don't recall meeting a Salisbury, I'm afraid."

"Oh, but of course, that's not his name, that's his title, the Marquis of Salisbury. His real name is Robert Gascoyne-Cecil. You may have met him or any number of his children, Lady Beatrix, Lady Gwendolyn, James, the Viscount Cranborne, Lord William Cecil, Lord Robert Cecil, Lord Edward Cecil, and Lord Hugh Cecil, as well as his nephews on the Balfour side of the family."

"Sounds like quite a brood, Mr. Holmes. Seems to me I may have run across one or two Cecils in my travels. Balfour sounds familiar too. I believe I saw a Balfour as a bowler in a cricket match once. I remember thinking, at the time, that if it were a baseball game, it would be a most unfortunate name for a pitcher."

"Well, I'm sure any impression they may have made would be in your notes. At least should be, if there was anything interesting at all in your encounters," replied Holmes.

"I'll muddle it around my brains for a bit. There may be something there and it certainly wouldn't hurt British sales if I could include a bit of the English aristocracy."

I could barely restrain myself from laughter at Holmes ploy. The one thing that Mycroft's agents couldn't control were the memories in Clemens' head. If there were any, and he chose to include them, Mycroft certainly could not be blamed. Perhaps a member of the privileged class would get a much deserved comeuppance. I gave Holmes a hint of a smile and a nod, acknowledging that I was pleased with his sense of justice.

"Excellent!" Holmes replied to the author. "Watson," he said, taking my arm and steering me toward the door before my righteous laughter bubbled over, "we must be off! Our business cannot wait a moment longer." Turning back to our client he added, "Mr. Clemens, it has been a genuine pleasure. Be sure to let me know if anything is missing. Enjoy your stay in England!"

"Goodbye, Sam," I cried over my shoulder. "I look forward to your next book!"

"And I yours, Doc," replied the American with a wave of his cigar.

Once outside I let out the laugh that had threatened to expose all in Clemens' presence.

"Holmes, that was delightful!" I finally managed as we deposited ourselves into a cab and Holmes called out 'Simpson's Restaurant' to the driver. "Surely if anything stirs in Clemens' memory he can now include it freely."

"We shall see, Watson. It may be that whatever Clemens may have witnessed is not worthy to be in his autobiography. But, we have planted a seed and its growth is not our concern."

"Well, if it's not worthy of Mark Twain to comment upon, then it's unlikely to be significant." I replied. "At any rate, I thank you for that seed. Perhaps it will grow into a thorn in some overbearing aristocrat's side."

"Or at least confound those branches of government whose meddling is beyond their purview" he answered. "Now I suggest we concentrate on an excellent meal."

"A Salisbury steak, perhaps?" I posed.

Holmes pulled his hat down over his eyes and refused to utter another word for the remainder of our trip.

Epilogue

Clemens' various engagements kept him on the move and we would not see him again before he left London for other performances. We did each receive some rather generous compensation, however. He rewarded Holmes, for solving the case, and me, for my assistance in both the case and in the medical care of his daughter. In his correspondence he included a generous offer to publish any future stories of mine in America, whether or not they were about Holmes' adventures.

A few months later, on a fine Summer day, I arose late one morning and found Holmes finishing off his breakfast with newspaper in hand.

"Good morning, Watson," he called. "I trust you enjoyed your concert with the widow Savage last night."

"The Symphony was excellent, Holmes, as was Adelaide's company."

"I perceived as much from your late return," he replied matter-of-factly.

I smiled in response, sat down and examined the remains of the breakfast offering provided by Mrs. Hudson. Deciding to forgo the cold eggs, I split and buttered a muffin and filled it with some bacon slices, in effect creating a sandwich of sorts. Having that and some tea to fortify me, I began my own perusal of the morning papers.

I noticed an item in the *Times* and relayed the information to my friend.

"Holmes, it says here that Sam Clemens has relocated to Dollis Hill House as the guest of Hugh Gilzean-Reid, the editor of the Edinburgh Weekly News."

"Well, that should lead to some lively discussions," replied Holmes. "When he was in Parliament, Gilzean-

-Reid was well known for his liberal views. I believe his wife is currently serving as President of the Women's Liberal Association."

"That indeed should create a wondrous forum for debate," I responded. "There's a situation that cries out for the proverbial fly on the wall."

Holmes selected a churchwarden from among his pipes, filled it with his favourite shag and deliberated as he set a match to it, "Well, perhaps some of those discussions will find their way into Gilzean-Reid's newspaper. I should certainly be surprised if he did not take advantage of having 'Mark Twain' under his own roof."

I nodded in agreement and returned to my reading as I finished my tea. A few moments later, though, Holmes spoke again.

"Speaking of our famous author client, Watson, I have been weighing one of his early remarks to us for some time now."

"Really?" I answered. "What would that be, Holmes?"

"At our first meeting he accused me of denying you your gift for words. I confess that statement has struck a spark of guilt that I cannot extinguish in good conscience as your friend."

"Your reasons have always been quite clear." I replied, "I have accepted the fact that my publications of your cases could have an adverse impact on your time for important work."

"And I appreciate your consideration of my position, old friend. But I think the time has come to put your talents back into exercise."

I could hardly believe my ears. Holmes had been unshakable in his position for years. I questioned him with barely controlled excitement.

"Are you quite sure about this?"

"For now, Doctor" he replied. "However, I would ask you to confine your reporting to those cases that occurred before Reichenbach, if convenient. I can certainly assist with any questions you might have, to fill in the gaps from those old notes of yours."

Astounded, I stammered. "That's very gracious of you, old boy. I always thought that the Baskerville Case would appeal to the public."

Holmes furrowed his brow and considered this, then replied. "Well, if Sir Henry has no objection, I suppose there were enough elements of detection and deduction to make a good lesson for the criminal scientist. Certainly your readers will enjoy the sensational aspect of the legendary hellhound. Let me know if you need any of my private case notes.[1]"

With that extraordinary statement, spoken so matter-of-factly, the legendary detective returned to his pipe and his paper, seeking out possibilities for his next case.

*****

Mark Twain once cautioned, "Keep away from people who try to belittle your ambitions. Small people always do that, but the really great make you feel that you, too, can become great."

---

[1] *The Hound of the Baskervilles* would be published in the *Strand* magazine in serialized form from August 1901 until April 1902.

Lightning Source UK Ltd.
Milton Keynes UK
UKHW020159010919
348896UK00015B/839/P